SHE WAS A KEY PIECE
OF THE PUZZLE,

AND A BEAUTIFUL PIECE . . .

She swayed across the rug like a dancer, her tight little behind jiggling seductively in the blue silk pajama bottoms. Detective Arthur Brown tried not to notice. He was on business, after all . . .

> *"We have good reason to believe," he said stiffly, "that the fragment in the dead man's hand was part of a larger photograph showing the location of the stolen money. We also have good reason to believe that you have another piece of that picture. And we want it. It's as simple as that."*

"You ever been to bed with a white girl?" she asked suddenly.

"McBain has never been better!"—*Roanoke Times*

JIGSAW
An 87th Precinct Mystery

by Ed McBain

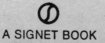

A SIGNET BOOK

NEW AMERICAN LIBRARY

SIGNET TRADEMARK REG. U.S. PAT. OFF. AND FOREIGN COUNTRIES
REGISTERED TRADEMARK—MARCA REGISTRADA
HECHO EN CHICAGO. U.S.A.

SIGNET, SIGNET CLASSIC, MENTOR, ONYX, PLUME, MERIDIAN and NAL BOOKS are published *in the United States* by
NAL PENGUIN INC.,
1633 Broadway, New York, New York 10019

FIRST SIGNET PRINTING, DECEMBER, 1970

5 6 7 8 9 10 11 12 13

PRINTED IN THE UNITED STATES OF AMERICA

This is for
HELEN AND GENE FEDERICO

1

DETECTIVE Arthur Brown did not like being called black.

This might have had something to do with his name, which was Brown. Or his color, which was also brown. Or it might have had something to do with the fact that when he was but a mere strip of a boy coming along in this fair city, the word "black" was usually linked alliteratively with the word "bastard." He was now thirty-four years old and somewhat old-fashioned, he supposed, but he still considered the word derogatory, no matter how many civil rights leaders endorsed it. Brown didn't need to seek identity in his color or in his soul. He searched for it in himself as a man, and usually found it there with ease.

He was six feet four inches tall, and he weighed two hundred and twenty pounds in his undershorts. He had the huge frame and powerful muscles of a heavyweight fighter, a square clean look emphasized by the way he wore his hair, clipped close, clinging to his skull like a soft black cap, a style he had favored even before it became fashionable to look "natural." His eyes were brown, his nostrils were large, he had thick lips and thicker hands, and he wore a .38 Smith & Wesson in a shoulder holster under his jacket.

The two men lying on the floor at his feet were white. And dead.

One of them was wearing black shoes, blue socks, dark blue trousers, a pale blue shirt open at the throat, a tan poplin zippered jacket, a gold Star-of-David on a slender gold chain around his neck, and two bullet holes in his chest. The other one was dressed more elegantly— brown shoes, socks and trousers, white shirt, green tie, houndstooth-check sports jacket. The broken blade of a switch knife was barely visible in his throat, just below the Adam's apple. A Luger was on the floor near his open right hand.

The apartment was a shambles.

It was not a great apartment to begin with; Brown had certainly seen better apartments, even in the ghetto where he had spent the first twenty-two years of his life. This one was on the third floor of a Culver Avenue tenement, two rooms and a bathroom, rear exposure, meaning that it faced on a back yard with clotheslines flapping Wednesday's wash. It was now close to 10 P.M., six minutes after the building's landlady had stopped the cop on the beat to say she had heard shots upstairs, four minutes after the patrolman had forced the door, found the stiffs, and called the station house. Brown, who had been catching, took the squeal.

The Homicide cops had not yet arrived, which was just as well. Brown could never understand the depart- ment regulation that made it mandatory for Homicide to check in on every damn murder committed in this city, even though the case was invariably assigned to the precinct answering the call. He found most Homicide cops grisly and humorless. His wife, Caroline, was fond of telling him that he himself was not exactly a very comical fellow, but Brown assumed that was merely a case of the prophet going unappreciated in his native land. In fact, *he* thought he was hilarious at times. As now, for example, when he turned to the police photogra- pher and said, "I wonder who did the interior decorating here." The police photographer apparently shared Caro- line Brown's opinion. Without cracking a smile, he did his little dance around the two corpses, snapping, twist- ing for another angle, snapping again, shifting now to this side of the dead men, now to the other, while Brown waited for his laugh.

"I said . . ." Brown said.

"I heard you, Artie," the photographer said, and clicked his camera again.

"This is certainly not the Taj Mahal," Brown said.

"Hardly anything is," the photographer answered.

"What are you so grumpy about?" Brown asked.

"Me? Grumpy? Who's grumpy?"

"Nobody," Brown said. He glanced at the corpses again, and then walked to the far side of the room, where two windows overlooked the back yard. One of the windows was wide open. Brown checked the latch on it, and saw immediately that it had been forced. Okay, he thought, that's how one of them got in. I wonder which one. And I also wonder *why*. What did he expect to steal in this dump?

Brown leaned over the window sill. There was nothing but an empty milk carton, a crumpled wad of waxed paper, and a flower pot on the fire escape outside. The flower pot had a dead plant in it. Brown looked down into the yard below. A woman was dumping her garbage into one of the cans adjacent to the alley wall. She accidentally dropped the lid of the can, clearly and resoundingly said, "Oh, shit!" and stooped to retrieve it. Brown turned away from the window.

Monoghan and Monroe, the detectives from Homicide, were just coming through the doorway. They were dressed almost identically, both wearing blue serge confirmation suits, brown shoes, and gray fedoras. Monroe was wearing a maroon knit tie. Monoghan wore a yellow silk tie. Their shields were pinned to the breast pockets of their suit jackets. Monroe had recently begun growing a mustache, and the sparse collection of hairs over the lip seemed to embarrass him. He kept blowing his nose into his handkerchief, even though he didn't have a cold, as though trying to hide his unsightly brush behind the white cotton square. Monoghan seemed even more embarrassed by the mustache than Monroe did. It seemed to him that after fifteen years of working together with a man, the man should not suddenly start growing a mustache one morning without first consulting his partner. Monoghan hated Monroe's mustache. He considered it unesthetic. It embarrassed him. It offended his eye. And because it offended his eye, he constantly stared at it. And the more often he stared at it, the more often Monroe took out his handkerchief and blew his nose, hiding his mustache.

"Well, well, what have we got here?" Monroe said, blowing his nose. "Hello, Brown."

"Hello, Brown," Monoghan said.

"Now this is what I call a thorough job," Monroe said,

pocketing his handkerchief. "Whoever went through this place was an expert."

"A professional," Monoghan said.

"It almost looks like the *police* shook it down."

"Or the firemen," Monoghan said, and looked at his partner's mustache. Monroe took out his handkerchief again.

"Must have wanted something pretty bad," he said, and blew his nose.

"What could anybody want in *this* joint?" Monoghan asked. "You know what you find in a joint like this?"

"What?" Brown asked.

"Cockroaches," Monoghan said.

"Bedbugs," Monroe added.

"Cockroaches and bedbugs," Monoghan summarized.

Monroe put away his handkerchief.

"*Look* at this joint," Monoghan said, and shook his head.

Brown looked at the joint. The bed had been stripped, the mattress slashed on both sides, cotton batting strewn all over the floor. The same thorough job had been done on the bed pillows and on the seat cushion, arms and back of the single easy chair in the room. Fade-marks on the walls showed where several framed prints had been hanging, but the pictures had been yanked down, their backs probably examined, and then thrown carelessly onto the floor. The contents of all the dresser drawers were similarly tossed all over the room, and the drawers themselves had been pulled out of the dresser and then flung aside. The one floor lamp in the room, overturned, had had its shade removed and discarded. Through the bathroom doorway, Brown could see the open medicine cabinet, its contents thrown into the sink. The top of the toilet tank had been taken off. Even the toilet paper had been removed from its roller. In the kitchen, the refrigerator door was open, and food had been hurled haphazardly onto the floor. The one drawer in the kitchen table had been emptied onto the white enamel tabletop, utensils scattered everywhere. As Monroe had wisely commented, someone must have wanted something pretty bad.

"You know who the stiffs are?" Monoghan asked Brown.

"Not yet."

"You figure it for an interrupted burglary?"

"Right."

"How'd he get in?"

"Through the fire escape window. Tool marks on the frame."

"Other guy came home unexpectedly, and *bingo!*"

"Think he got what he came after?"

"Haven't checked him out," Brown said.

"What're you waiting for?"

"Lou's still taking pictures. And the M.E. isn't here yet."

"Who reported the crime?" Monroe asked.

"The landlady. She heard shots, stopped Kiely on the beat."

"Get her up here," Monoghan said.

"Right," Brown answered. He went to the door, told the patrolman there to go get the landlady, and then saw Marshall Davies hurrying down the hallway toward the apartment.

"I'm sorry I'm late, Artie," he said. "I had a goddamn flat."

"There was a call for you," Brown said.

"Who from?"

"Lieutenant Grossman."

"What'd he want?"

"Said you should go right back to the lab."

"The lab? What for? Who's going to handle *this* if I go back to the lab?"

"Don't know," Brown said.

"You know what he's probably got waiting for me downtown? Some nice little surprise, that's what. Some nice hit-and-run victim. Some guy who got run over by a trailer truck. I'll be down there picking headlight splinters out of his ass all night. Boy oh boy, what a day."

"It's hardly started," Brown said.

"It started for me at seven o'clock this morning," Davies said. He sighed heavily. "Okay, I'm heading back. If he should call again, tell him I'm on my way. I don't know who's going to handle this for you, Artie. The M.E. been here yet?"

"No, not yet."

"Situation normal," Davies said, and walked out.

The patrolman came upstairs with the landlady not five minutes later. By that time, the Assistant Medical Examiner had arrived and was checking out the corpses. Brown and the two Homicide detectives took the landlady into the kitchen, where they could talk to her without the fascinating distraction of two bodies lying on the floor. She was a woman in her late forties, not unattractive, her blond hair pulled into a bun at the back of her head. She had wide Irish eyes, as green as County Cork, and she spoke with the faintest hint of a brogue. Her name was Mrs. Walter Byrnes.

"No kidding?" Monoghan said. "You any relation to the lieutenant?"

"What lieutenant?"

"Runs the Eight-seven," Monroe said.

"The Eighty-seventh squad," Monoghan said.

"He's a cop," Monroe said.

"I'm not related to any cops," Mrs. Byrnes said.

"He's a very good cop," Monoghan said.

"I'm not related to him," Mrs. Byrnes said, firmly.

"You want to tell us what happened, Mrs. Byrnes?" Monroe said.

"I heard shots. I went right outside and yelled for the police."

"Did you come up here?"

"Nope."

"Why not?"

"Would *you?*"

"Mrs. Byrnes," Brown said, "when you came in just now, did you happen to notice the bodies in the other room?"

"I'd have to be deaf, dumb, and blind not to, wouldn't I?" she said.

"Do you know either of those two men?"

"One of them, yes."

"Which one?"

"The one wearing the sports jacket," she said. Unflinchingly, she added, "The one with the knife blade sticking out of his throat."

"And who is he, Mrs. Byrnes?"

"His name is Donald Renninger. He's been living here in the building for more than two years."

"And the other man? The one wearing the Jewish star?"

"Never saw him before in my life."

"He's the one who broke in, I guess," Monroe said.

"We've had a *lot* of burglaries around here," Mrs. Byrnes said, and looked at the detectives reproachfully.

"Well, we try to do our best," Monoghan said dryly.

"Sure you do," Mrs. Byrnes said, even more dryly.

"Any idea what Mr. Renninger did for a living?" Brown asked.

"He worked at a filling station."

"Would you know where?"

"In Riverhead someplace. I don't know exactly where."

"Is he married?"

"No."

"He was a bachelor, right?" Monroe asked.

"If he wasn't married, why yes, I guess he was a bachelor," Mrs. Byrnes said sarcastically, and then looked at Monroe's mustache.

Monroe took out his handkerchief. Apologetically, he blew his nose and said, "He *could* have been divorced."

"That's true," Monoghan said.

Monroe smiled at him, and put away his handkerchief.

"But you never saw the other man?" Brown said.

"Never."

"Not here in the building . . ."

"No."

". . . or in the neighborhood either?"

"No place," she said.

"Thank you, Mrs. Byrnes."

The landlady went to the door. She turned before she went out, and said, "What's his first name?"

"Whose?"

"The lieutenant's?"

"Peter."

"We don't have a Peter Byrnes in our family," she said, and went out, satisfied.

The M.E. was finished with the bodies. As he passed the detectives, he said, "We'll give you written reports soon as the autopsies are made. You want some guesses for now?"

"Sure," Brown said.

"Looks like the first bullet hit the guy in the poplin jacket a little low, probably got deflected off a rib. Anyway, it didn't stop him right away. Left fist is clenched, he probably threw a punch and still had time to stick his knife in the other guy's throat, probably just as the gun went off a second time. *That* shot went clear through the heart, I'd guess. The guy in the poplin jacket started to drop, and the knife blade broke off as he fell. The other guy went down, too, probably died within minutes. Looks to me as if the knife caught his jugular, awful lot of blood in there. Okay?"

"Okay, thanks," Brown said.

"You handling this, Artie?"

"Looks like I'm stuck with it."

"Well, it's open and shut. I'll get the reports up to you tomorrow morning, that soon enough?"

"Nobody's going any place," Brown said.

"Toodle-oo," the M.E. said, and waggled his fingers and went out.

"So what'd the burglar *want* here?" Monoghan asked.

"Maybe *this*," Monroe said. He was crouched near the corpse in the poplin jacket. He pried open the dead man's clenched left hand to reveal what appeared to be a portion of a glossy photograph clutched into the palm. He lifted the photo scrap and handed it to Brown. "Take a look at it," he said.

2

"WHAT IS IT?" Detective Steve Carella asked.

"Piece of a snapshot," Brown said.

They were in a corner of the squadroom, Brown sitting behind his desk, Carella perched on one end of it. Early morning June sunshine streamed into the office. A mild breeze filtered through the wire grilles covering the open windows. Carella, sitting on the edge of the desk, sniffed of the late spring air, and wished he were sleeping in the park someplace. A tall, wiry man with wide shoulders and narrow hips, he gave the impression of being an athlete in training, even though the last time he'd engaged in any sportlike activity was the snorkeling he'd done in Puerto Rico on his last vacation. Unless one wished to count the various footraces he had run with criminals of every stripe and persuasion. Carella did not like to count those. A man could get winded just counting those. He brushed a strand of longish brown hair off his forehead now, squinted his brown eyes at the photo scrap, and wondered if he needed glasses.

"What does it look like to you?" he asked.

"A dancing girl in a leotard," Brown answered.

"Looks more like a bottle of Haig & Haig Pinch to me." Carella said. "What do you suppose this furry stuff is?"

"What furry stuff?"

"This textured stuff, whatever-the-hell-it-is."

15

"Mud, I would guess."

"Or part of a wall. A stucco wall." Carella shrugged, and dropped the scrap onto the desktop. "You really think this is why . . . *what's* his name?"

"According to the identification in his wallet, his name was Eugene Edward Ehrbach."

"Ehrbach. Anything on him?"

"I'm running a check with the I.B. right now. On *both* of them."

"You think Ehrbach really broke into the apartment to get *this?*" Carella asked, and tapped the photograph segment with a pencil.

"Well, why else would it be in his hand, Steve? I can't see him going up there with a piece of a snapshot in his hand, can you?"

"I guess not."

"Anyway, I'll tell you the truth, I don't see as it makes a hell of a lot of difference. The M.E. said it's open and shut, and I'm inclined to agree with him. Ehrbach broke into the apartment, Renninger suddenly came home and surprised him, and we get a neat double homicide."

"And the photograph?"

"Well, let's say Ehrbach *was* after it. So what? He could just as easily have been after Renninger's wrist watch. Either way, they're both dead. The snapshot doesn't change the disposition of the case either way."

"No, it doesn't."

"Soon as we get those autopsy reports, I'm going to type this up as closed. You see any other way?"

"No, it looks pretty clear."

"M.E. promised them for this morning." Brown looked at his watch. "Well, it's still a little early."

"I wonder what kind of customers we're dealing with here," Carella said.

"How do you mean?"

"Two nice ordinary citizens, one of them carrying a Luger, and the other one carrying a switch knife with an eight-inch blade."

"Whatever Ehrbach was, he wasn't a nice ordinary citizen. He opened that window like a pro."

"And Renninger?"

"Landlady says he worked at a filling station."

"I wish the I.B. would get off its dead ass," Carella said.

"Why?"

"I'm curious."

"Let's say they *have* got records," Brown said. "It still wouldn't change anything, would it?"

"You sound anxious to close this out," Carella said.

"I got a caseload up to my eyeballs, but that's not why I want to close it. There's just no reason to keep it *open*," Brown said.

"Unless there was a third party in that apartment," Carella said.

"There's no indication of that, Steve."

"Or unless . . ."

"Unless what?"

"I don't know. But why would anyone risk a burglary rap just to get a piece of a snapshot?"

"Excuse me," a voice called from across the squad-room. Both detectives turned simultaneously toward the slatted wooden railing at the far end of the office. A tall hatless man in a gray nailhead suit stood just out-side the gate. He was perhaps thirty-five years old, with a thatch of black hair and a thick black handle-bar mustache that would have caused serious pangs of envy in someone like Monroe. His eyebrows were thick and black as well, raised now in polite inquiry over startlingly blue eyes that glinted in the squadroom sunshine. His speech stamped him immediately as a native of the city, with not a little trace of Calm's Pointese in it. "The desk sergeant said I should come right up," he said. "I'm look-ing for Detective Brown."

"That's me," Brown said.

"Okay to come in?"

"Come ahead."

The man searched briefly for the latch on the inside of the gate, found it, and strode into the office. He was a big man with big hands, the left one clutched around the handle of a dispatch case. He held the case very tightly. Brown had the feeling it should have been chained to his wrist. Smiling pleasantly, he extended his right hand and said, "Irving Krutch. Nice to meet you." His teeth were dazzling, the smile framed by a pair of dimples, one on either side of his mouth. He had high cheekbones, and a straight unbroken nose, and he looked like the lead in an Italian Western. The only thing he needed to attain instant stardom on the silver screen, Brown thought, was a change of name. Irving Krutch did nothing for his image. Steve Stunning, Hal Handsome, Geoff Gorgeous, any of those might have suited him better.

"How do you do?" Brown said, and took his hand

briefly. He did not bother introducing Carella; cops rarely observed such formalities during business hours.

"Okay to sit down?" Krutch said.

"Please," Brown said, and indicated a chair to the right of his desk. Krutch sat. Carefully preserving the knife-crease in his trousers, he crossed his legs, and unleashed the dazzling smile again.

"So," he said, "looks like you've got yourselves a little murder, huh?"

Neither of the cops answered him. They *always* had themselves a little murder, and they weren't in the habit of discussing homicides, little or otherwise, with strange, handsome, mustached, well-dressed smiling civilians who barged into the squadroom.

"The two guys over on Culver Avenue," Krutch said. "I read about them in the paper this morning."

"What about them?" Brown asked.

"I guess I should tell you I'm an insurance investigator," Krutch said. "Trans-American Insurance."

"Mm-huh," Brown said.

"Do you know the company?"

"The name sounds familiar."

"I've been with them for twelve years now, started there when I got out of college." He paused, then added, "Princeton." He waited for some response, saw that mention of his illustrious alma mater was not generating too much excitement, and then said, "I've worked with this squad before. Detective named Meyer Meyer. He still with you?"

"He's still with us," Brown said.

Carella, who had been silent until now, said, "What were you working on?"

"The National Savings & Loan Association holdup," Krutch said. "Six years ago."

"In what capacity?"

"I told you. I'm an insurance investigator. They're one of our clients." He smiled again. "Took us for a bundle on that one."

The men were silent again.

"So?" Brown said at last.

"So," Krutch said, "I read about your two corpses in the paper this morning, and I thought I'd better get up here right away."

"Why?"

"Lend you a hand," Krutch said, smiling. "Or maybe vice versa."

"You know something about those killings?" Brown asked.

"Yep."

"What do you know?"

"The newspaper said you found a piece of a photograph in Ehrbach's hand," Krutch said. His blue eyes shifted dramatically toward the photo scrap lying on Brown's desk. "Is that it?"

"What about it?" Brown said.

"I've got another piece. And if you shake down Ehrbach's pad, I'm pretty sure you'll find a *third* piece."

"Do you want to tell it, or do we have to pull teeth?"

"I'm ready to tell it."

"Then tell it."

"Sure. Will you help me?"

"To do what?"

"First, to get the piece in Ehrbach's place."

"Why do you want it?"

"Three pieces are better than one, no?"

"Look, Mr. Krutch," Brown said, "if you've got something to say, say it. Otherwise, it's been nice meeting you, and I hope you sell a lot of insurance policies."

"I don't sell insurance, I investigate claims."

"Fine. I wish you lots of luck. Yes or no? Shit or get off the pot."

Krutch smiled at Carella, as though sharing with him his aversion to such crude language. Carella ignored the smile. He was agreeing with Brown. He hated coy disclosures. The 87th Squad ran a nice little store up here on the second floor of the building, and so far the only thing Krutch was spending in it was time. *Their* time.

Sensing the impatience of the two detectives, Krutch said, "Let me fill you in."

"Please do," Brown said.

"Fade in," Krutch said. "Six . . ."

"What?" Brown asked.

"That's a movie expression. Fade in."

"You involved with movies?" Brown asked, ready to confirm the suspicion he'd harbored from the moment Krutch walked in.

"No."

"Then why the movie expression?"

"Everybody says 'Fade in,' " Krutch explained.

"I don't say 'Fade in,' " Brown replied.

"Okay, so we *won't* fade in," Krutch said, and shrugged. "Six years ago, in this city, in broad daylight on a rainy afternoon in August, four men held up the Culver Avenue branch of N.S.L.A. and got away with seven hundred and fifty thousand dollars. That's a lot of kale. The branch, incidentally, is located in this precinct."

"Go on," Carella said.

"You remember the case now?" Krutch asked. "Meyer and O'Brien were working on it."

"I remember it," Carella said. "Go ahead."

"Do *you* remember it, Detective Brown?"

"Yes," Brown said.

"I don't think I got your name," Krutch said, turning to Carella.

"Carella."

"Nice to meet you. Are you Italian?"

"Yes."

"The leader of the gang was Italian. Fellow named Carmine Bonamico, record as long as your arm. In fact, he'd just got out of Castleview after serving a five-and-dime there. First thing he did, while he was still on parole, was knock over the bank. You remember any of this?"

"I remember *all* of it," Carella said.

"Are my facts correct so far?"

"They are."

"My facts are *always* correct," Krutch said, and smiled. Nobody smiled with him. "The wheelman was a young punk named Jerry Stein, a Jewish kid from Riverhead, his first job. The two guns were both ex-cons, Lou D'Amore from Majesta and Pete Ryan, also from Riverhead, a regular little United Nations they had on that job. They came in just before closing time, grabbed as much as they could from the vault, shot one of the tellers, and then drove off, presumably heading for Calm's Point, which is where Bonamico lived with his wife. It was raining; did I mention it was raining?"

"You mentioned it."

"They got onto the River Road, and had almost reached the Calm's Point Bridge, when the car went into a skid, hit another car, and caused a traffic tie-up. Two patrolmen from the Three-six pulled up in a squad car, and Bonamico and his pals opened fire. All four of them were killed inside of five minutes. The great mystery is why they began shooting at all. The car was clean. It was later searched from top to bottom, but the bank loot wasn't in it. Not a dime of it." Krutch paused. "Okay, dissolve . . ."

Brown looked at him.

"Trans-American gets called in, Irving Krutch investigating." He grinned. "That's me. Result? Two years of intensive search for that money, and no trace of it. We finally settled the claim in full, seven hundred and fifty G's from our coffers to N.S.L.A.'s." Krutch paused. "That's bad. I don't have to tell you how bad that is."

"How bad is it?" Brown asked.

"Bad. Bad for Trans-American, and especially bad for Irving Krutch who couldn't find the money. Irving Krutch was up for a promotion at the time. Instead, Irving Krutch is now handling minor claims, at the same salary he was getting six years ago. Krutch is an ambitious fellow. He doesn't like dead-end jobs."

"Why doesn't Krutch *change* his job?" Carella suggested.

"Because the field's a narrow one, and losing seven hundred and fifty thousand dollars is the kind of word that gets around very fast. Besides, Krutch has an inordinate amount of pride in his work."

"Do you always talk about yourself in the third person?" Carella asked. "Like your own biographer?"

"It helps me to be objective. It's hard to be objective about losing seven hundred and fifty thousand dollars for the company, especially when the case has been officially closed by your squad."

"Who told you that?" Carella said.

"You got the thieves, didn't you?"

"The case is still in our Open File."

"How come?"

"Let's say we *also* have an inordinate amount of pride in our work," Carella said. "The money wasn't in the car. Okay, the River Road is some three miles from the bank. Which means that somewhere along the escape route, the money could have changed hands. If that happened, then the rest of the gang is still at large, just itching to spend all that cash. We'd like to get them."

"Forget it."

"What do you mean?"

"The money wasn't turned over to *anybody.* If you're keeping the case open in hope of finding the rest of the gang, forget it. There were only four of them, and they're all dead."

"Do you know that for a fact?"

"Yes. I got it from Bonamico's sister-in-law." Krutch paused. "You mind if I tell it in order?"

"Any order you like," Brown said, "so long as you *tell* it."

"Okay, dissolve. Krutch is still bugged by the loss of that money. It keeps him awake nights. His company has settled the claim, not to mention his future, but it still bugs him. Where can the money be? Who's got it? Bonamico is no master criminal, mind you, but neither is he stupid enough to throw that kind of cash out the window of a getaway car. So where the hell is it? Krutch keeps wondering about it. Krutch keeps tossing and turning at night . . ."

"Krutch should be writing mystery stories," Carella said.

". . . obsessed with the thought of locating that cash and becoming a contender again."

"A contender?"

"At Trans-American."

"Oh, I thought maybe you also did a little boxing on the side," Brown said.

"Matter of fact, I used to box in the Navy," Krutch said. "Middleweight division." He paused, eyed them both shrewdly, and said, "You guys don't like me much, do you?"

"We're civil servants," Brown said, "soliciting information from a private citizen who may or may not possess knowledge of a crime. We are patiently waiting. If we have to wait much longer, we'll be forced to rent you office space."

"I like your sense of humor," Krutch said, and smiled.

"My wife doesn't," Brown said. "We're still waiting, Mr. Krutch. We are getting old and gray waiting."

"Okay. Two months ago, I got lucky."

"You mean you were still working on this thing?"

"Not officially. Only on my own time. Pride, remember? Ambition. Tenacity. Krutch the would-be contender. I opened the paper one morning two months ago and learned that a woman named Alice Bonamico had died of cancer at the Sacred Heart Hospital in Calm's Point. No one would have noticed her passing, of course, if she hadn't incidentally been the widow of one Carmine Bonamico who had knocked over a bank six years earlier and caused the loot to magically disappear. I knew the lady because I'd talked to her often when I was investigating the claim. She was a nice type, quiet, pretty in a dark Sicilian way, you'd never think she'd been married to a cheap hood. Anyway, the newspaper item said that she was survived by a sister named Lucia Feroglio. I made a mental note, and later discovered she was a spinster, also living in Calm's Point."

"How much later was this?"

"A week or so. As soon as Alice Bonamico's will was filed in Surrogate's Court. It was a very interesting will. Aside from leaving her entire estate to her sister Lucia, it also left her, and I quote, 'Certain mementos, documents, photographs, and photographic segments considered to be of value by the deceased.' I immediately got on my horse and went to visit Lucia Feroglio in Calm's Point."

"This was two months ago?"

"Right. The third day of April. A Friday. Lucia Feroglio is an old lady in her seventies, memory failing, barely speaking English, partially deaf. You ever try to talk to a deaf woman?"

Carella said nothing.

"Anyway, I talked to her. I convinced her that her brother-in-law had taken out a very small policy on his wife's life, naming Lucia Feroglio as beneficiary, and that a check for one thousand dollars would be issued to her as soon as the conditions of the policy were met. I invented the conditions, of course."

"What were they?"

"That she satisfy my company that she was indeed in possession of the 'Certain mementos, documents, photographs, and photographic segments considered to be of value by the deceased.' Even deaf old ladies who hardly speak English can understand a thousand dollars. She patiently went through all the crap her sister had left her—family pictures, birth certificates, even the caul Alice had been born with, carefully wrapped in a square of pink satin; that's supposed to be good luck, you know, if you're born with a caul. And in the midst of all this crap was exactly what I hoped would be there."

"Which was?"

"A list of names. Or at least a partial list of names. And a piece of a photograph." Krutch paused. "Would you like to see them?"

"Yes," Carella said.

Krutch opened his dispatch case. Resting on top of a sheaf of Trans-American claim forms was a legal-sized white envelope. Krutch opened the envelope and took out a scrap of paper. He put it on the desktop, and both detectives looked at it.

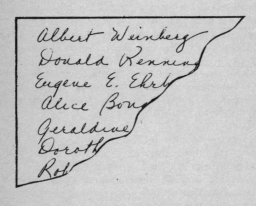

"Those names are in Carmine Bonamico's handwriting," Krutch said. "I'm quite familiar with it."

"Seven of them," Carella said.

"Or maybe more," Krutch answered. "As you can see, the list is torn."

"How'd it get torn?"

"I don't know. That's the way Lucia turned it over to me. It may have been accidentally damaged, or another piece of it may be in someone else's hands. Considering what Bonamico did with the photograph, that's a likely possibility."

"Let's see the picture," Carella said.

Krutch dipped into the envelope again. He took out a piece of a glossy photograph and put it on the desktop, alongside the scrap they had found clutched in Ehrbach's hand.

"How do we know these are pieces of the same photograph?" Carella asked.

"They're both cut like a jigsaw puzzle," Krutch said. "That can't be accidental. Nor can it be accidental that you found *your* piece in the hand of one of the men listed here in Bonamico's handwriting. Or that the *other* dead man is *also* on the list." Krutch paused. "Ehrbach's a better burglar than I am. I've been in and out of Renninger's place a dozen times in the past two months, and I never found a thing."

"You're admitting to breaking and entry, Mr. Krutch?"

"Shall I send for my lawyer?" Krutch asked, and grinned.

"Did you shake down Ehrbach's place as well?"

"I did. And found nothing. *His* piece is probably as carefully hidden as Renninger's was."

Carella looked at the list again. "Who's Albert Weinberg?"

"One of Stein's close buddies. Jerry Stein, the kid who drove the getaway car. Beginning to make sense?"

"Not much."

"Weinberg's a hood in his own right. So are the other two, in case you don't already know."

"Which other two?"

"Renninger and Ehrbach. Renninger was busted eight years ago for pushing junk. He was in Caramoor at the time of the holdup, got out of prison only two years ago. Ehrbach was busted twice for burglary, one more time and they'd have thrown away the key. Makes the risk he took seem even more meaningful, doesn't it? He was taking the chance of a third fall, and for what? Unless that picture means something, he was a goddam fool to break into Renninger's place."

"You're better than the I.B.," Brown said. "Assuming this is straight goods."

"As I told you," Krutch said, smiling, "my facts are *always* correct."

"What about the other names on this list?"

"I've been through the telephone book a hundred times. You know how many Geraldines there are? Don't ask. As for Dorothy, she could be Dorothy *Anybody*. And the R-o-b? That could be Robert, or Roberta, or Robin, or even Robespierre, who knows? It was easy to fill in the 'Renninger' because the name was almost complete. And I doped out the 'Ehrbach' because of the 'Eugene E.' They're both listed in the Isola directory. Alice is Alice Bonamico, of course. But I have no idea who the others are, and no idea whether there are more than seven. I hope not. *Seven* pieces of a puzzle are more than enough."

"And when you assemble this puzzle, Mr. Krutch, what then?"

"When I assemble this puzzle," Krutch said, "I will have the exact location of the seven hundred and fifty thousand dollars stolen from N.S.L.A. six years ago."

"How do you know that?"

"Lucia Feroglio told me. Oh, it took some time to get it out of her, believe me. As I told you, her memory is failing, and she's partially deaf, and her English is of the *Mama mia* variety. But she *finally* remembered that her sister had told her the photograph showed where the treasure was. That was the exact word she used. Treasure."

"She said that in English?" Carella asked. "She said 'treasure'?"

"No. She said *tesoro*. In Italian."

"Maybe she was only calling you 'darling,' " Carella said.

"I doubt it."

"You speak Italian, do you?"

"A girlfriend of mine told me what it meant. *Tesoro*. Treasure."

"So now there are two pieces," Brown said. "What do you want from us?"

"I want you to help me find the other *five* pieces. Or however many more there are." Krutch smiled. "I'm getting too well known, you see. Toward the end there, both Renninger and Ehrbach knew I was on to them. I wouldn't be surprised if Ehrbach *got* to Renninger merely by tailing *me*."

"You make it sound very complicated, Mr. Krutch."

"It *is* complicated. I'm sure that Weinberg knows I've been watching *him*, too. And frankly, I can't risk getting busted on a burglary rap. Which might happen if I keep breaking into places." He smiled again. The smile had lost none of its dazzle.

"So you want *us* to break into places for you, huh?"

"It's been done before."

"It's against the law, even for cops."

"*Lots* of things are against the law. There's seven hundred and fifty G's involved here. I'm sure the Eighty-seventh wouldn't mind locating it. Be quite a feather in your cap, after all these years."

"Yes, it might be," Carella said.

"So do it," Krutch said simply.

"Do *what?*" Brown asked.

"First of all, go over Ehrbach's place with a fine comb. You can do that legally. He's the victim of a homicide, and you're conducting an investigation."

"Okay, let's say we shake down Ehrbach's place."

"Yes, and you find the third piece of that picture."

"Assuming we do, *then* what?"

"Then you go after Weinberg."

"How? What's our legal excuse *there*, Krutch?"

"You don't have one. You couldn't approach him as fuzz, anyway. He's been in trouble before. He's not likely to co-operate with The Law."

"What kind of trouble?"

"Assault. He beat a woman half to death with his fists. He's enormous, must weigh at least two hundred and fifty pounds. He could break either one of you in half with just a dirty look, believe me." Krutch paused. "What do you say?"

"It might be worth our time," Carella said.

"We'll have to talk it over with the lieutenant."

"Yeah, you talk it over with him. I think *he* might understand how nice it would be to recover that bank loot." Krutch smiled again. "Meanwhile, I'll leave the list and the picture with you."

"Won't you need them?"

"I've got copies," Krutch said.

"How come somebody so smart needs our help?" Carella asked.

"That smart I ain't," Krutch said. He took a card from his wallet and placed it on the desk. "That's my home number," he said. "Don't try to reach me at Trans-American. Let me know what you decide."

"We will indeed," Carella said.

"Thank you," Krutch said. He offered his hand to Brown. "Detective Brown?" He retrieved his hand, shook hands next with Carella. "Detective Carella?" Then he smiled his dazzling smile and went out of the squadroom.

"What do you think?" Brown said.

"I don't know. What do *you* think?" Carella said.

"I don't know. Let's see what the lieutenant thinks."

3

Lieutenant Byrnes looked at the list of names, and then turned his attention to the two pieces of the photograph:

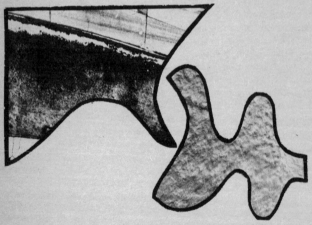

"Don't even look like they *belong* together," he muttered.

They had filled him in on Krutch's story, and he had listened intently, head cocked slightly to one side, blue eyes shifting from Carella's face to Brown's as they alternately picked up threads of the narrative. He was a thickset man, Byrnes, with heavy hands, the backs of

28

which were sprinkled with liver spots. His hair was going white, and he had a bald patch barely beginning to show at the back of his head. But there was a sense of contained power about him, the certain knowledge that he had broken many a hood's nose before being promoted to his present desk job. Impatiently, he looked at the photograph segments again, turning each one on his desktop, trying to fit them together, and then giving up the job.

"Guy comes in here with a story," Byrnes said, "what does he expect us to do? Drop everything and go on a goddamn treasure hunt?'

"Well," Carella said, "there's a possibility he's right."

"A pretty *slim* possibility, if you ask me. Where'd you say he got this story? From an old lady who hardly speaks English, right?"

"That's right."

"But she told him in Italian," Brown said. "She told him the picture shows where *il tresoro* is buried."

"*Il te*soro," Carella corrected.

"Did she say that? Buried?"

"No. I don't know. Hidden, I think she said. What'd she say, Steve?"

"Just that the picture shows where the treasure *is*, I think. That's all."

"She didn't say buried, huh?"

"I don't think so."

"I just hate to put a man on this, and then . . ." Byrnes shook his head. "It's not as if we've got nothing else to do around here, you know."

The detectives were silent.

"Let's say we search Ehrbach's place," Byrnes said. "And let's say we *do* find a third piece of this picture, then what?"

"Then Krutch's story begins to sound a little better," Carella said.

"Yes, but where do we go from there?" Byrnes asked. "I'm willing to put you on it . . . okay, we don't find anything, we've only wasted a day. But suppose we *do* find something, *then* what? This fellow . . . what's his name?" Byrnes consulted the list again. "Weinberg. Albert Weinberg. He's the next logical step. But Krutch says the man's got an assault record, which means he can smell The Law six blocks away. Whoever we send after him would have to use a cover, and I'd need a second man for a contact and drop. That's two men out

of action, maybe on a wild-goose chase." He shook his
head again. "I don't know." He looked down at the photograph segments and then up at Carella. "What's your
caseload like, Steve?"

"I've got that dry-cleaning store holdup, and the mug-
gings over on Ainsley . . . six in the past two weeks,
same m.o. I've also got a lead I want to run down on
the pusher who's been working the junior high school on
Seventeenth. And there're two cases coming to trial this
month. I have to be in court on Tuesday, matter of fact."

"What about you, Artie?"

"I forgot to mention . . ." Carella said.

"Yeah?"

"Couple of burglaries over in Smoke Rise. We've been
getting a lot of static on those because the sister of a
municipal judge lives in the neighborhood."

"Yeah, so let Hizzoner go find the burglar," Byrnes
said dryly. "Artie?"

"A hit-and-run, a jewelry store holdup, and a knifing.
I'm supposed to be in court tomorrow on the knifing.
It'll be a quick trial—the guy stabbed his wife when he
found her in bed with another man."

"You want to take a crack at this Weinberg character?
Assuming we find anything in Ehrbach's apartment?"

"Sure," Brown said.

"Does Weinberg live in the precinct? Would he be likely
to spot you as a cop?"

"I don't know."

"Check him out with the I.B., see if they've got an
address for him."

"Right."

"You'd better find out where he's operated, too, which
cities, and pick your cover accordingly. Don't make it
anything too big, Artie, don't say you're a mob gun from
Chicago or anything like that. Be too simple for him to
check if he's got any connections at all. Make it a numbers runner, a small-time pusher, something unimportant.
You stumbled on your piece of the picture, you think
Weinberg's got another piece, and you want to team up
with him. Keep it as simple as that."

"Right."

"Steve, you'll have to be the outside man at the skunk
works."

"Fine."

"Arrange a drop, and keep your contacts as few as
possible. This guy Weinberg doesn't sound like a customer

to fool around with. And let's not go overboard on this
thing, okay? Let's handle it in easy stages. If we don't
turn up anything at Ehrbach's place, that's it, back to the
salt mines. If we hit pay dirt, we move on to Weinberg,
stay with him a day or two. If it looks like he's got a
piece of the picture, we stick with him. Otherwise, we
thank Krutch for his information and we drop the whole
damn thing." He looked up at the two men. "Anything
else?"

"Just one thing," Carella said. "The I.B. called a few
minutes ago and verified everything Krutch said about
the two dead men."

"So?"

"So maybe he's right about what we'll find in Ehrbach's
apartment, too."

"Maybe," Byrnes said.

Judging from Eugene Edward Ehrbach's apartment, the
man had been a highly successful burglar. One could, of
course, argue that anyone who had already taken two
falls for burglary could not, by any stretch of the imagi-
nation, be considered a *successful* burglar. But the fact
remained that Ehrbach lived in a luxury apartment close
to Silvermine Oval; neither of the detectives who shook
down the place could have afforded anything even remotely similar to it on their salaries.

The doorman was not pleased to see them.

He had been hired to check on any and all strangers
entering the building, his job being to prevent tenants
from getting strangled in the elevator, and incidentally to
call taxis for them on rainy nights. It didn't matter that
these two strangers identified themselves as detectives
from the 87th Squad. The doorman liked detectives as
much as he liked stranglers or burglars. He had no way
of knowing, naturally, that Eugene Edward Ehrbach had
been a burglar, and undoubtedly a highly successful one.
He told the detectives that he would have to check with
the manager of the building, and even though they told
him they were investigating a murder, he insisted on making his telephone call. When he got off the phone, he said,
"It's okay, but don't go making a mess up there," which
was exactly what they *intended* to make up there.

Ehrbach had lived on the tenth floor of the building,
in an apartment at the end of the corridor. There were
three other apartments on the floor. Ehrbach's was the
choice apartment since it overlooked the River Harb.

There were two rivers flanking Isola, the Harb on the
north and the Dix on the south. Apartments overlooking
either of these waterways were considered very desirable,
even though the view of the next state across the Harb
featured a big housing development and the roller coaster
of an amusement park, and the view of the Dix revealed
a grimy gray hospital on an island, mid-river, a collection
of spiny bridges leading to Calm's Point and Sands Spit,
and a house of detention on another island out beyond
Devil's Causeway. From Ehrbach's living room window
(in addition to the roller coaster, the housing development, and an insistently blinking SPRY sign), you could
also see all the way uptown to the Hamilton Bridge.

Carella and Brown entered the apartment with a pass-
key provided by the doorman, and found themselves in a
carpeted foyer. Their reflected images looked back at
them from a gilt-framed mirror hanging on the wall facing the door. A long narrow table was against that wall,
just below the mirror. The apartment ran off to the right
and left of the foyer. They made a perfunctory check of
the place, discovering that there were four rooms in all:
living room, kitchen, den, and bedroom. A small bathroom was off the entrance foyer, and another bathroom
adjoined the bedroom. That was it, and very nice indeed.
They divided the apartment in half, Carella taking the
foyer, the small bathroom, the kitchen and the den;
Brown taking the bedroom, the living room, and the
second bathroom. With all the expertise and *sang-froid*
of a demolition crew, they started searching for the scrap
of photo Irving Krutch was certain Ehrbach had possessed. They began the job at noon. At midnight, they
were still looking.

They had made two trips downstairs for sandwiches
and coffee, Carella going out at 2 P.M. and Brown going
out at seven. Aside from slashing up the mattresses and
upholstered furniture, a license not granted to them, they
had done a thorough and painstaking job, but had found
nothing. They sat now in the living room, exhausted,
Brown in an easy chair near a standing floor lamp, Carella straddling the piano bench. The lamp was on, it cast
a warm and cozy glow over the moss-green wall-to-wall
carpeting.

"Maybe we ought to take it up," Brown said.

"Take what up?" Carella asked.

"The carpet."

"That's a big job."

"The way they lay this stuff," Brown said, "is they've got these strips of wood with tacks sticking up out of it. They nail that to the floor all around the room, and then hook the carpet onto it. You ever see these guys work?"

"Yeah," Carella said.

"You got wall-to-wall carpeting in your house?" Brown asked.

"No."

"Me, neither. A hood like Ehrbach has wall-to-wall carpeting, and all I've got is a ten-by-twelve in the living room. How do you figure it?"

"Guess we're in the wrong racket," Carella said. "Did you check out all these books?"

"Every page."

"How about the switch plates? Did you unscrew them?"

"Yep."

"Nothing scotch-taped to the backs, huh?"

"Nothing."

Carella glanced at the floor lamp. "Did you take off that shade?"

"Yeah, zero. It'd show, anyway, with the light on."

"That's right, yeah."

"How about the ball in the toilet tank?" Brown asked. "They're hollow, you know. He might have . . ."

"I pried it open," Carella said. "Nothing."

"Maybe we *ought* to take up this damn carpet," Brown said.

"Be here all night," Carella said. "If we have to do that, we'd better get a crew in tomorrow. Did you look in the piano?"

"Yeah, *and* the piano bench."

"How about the clock-radio in the bedroom?"

"Unscrewed the back. Nothing. The television in the den?"

"Same thing." Carella smiled. "Maybe we ought to do what my son does when he loses one of his toys."

"What does he do?"

"Well, he starts by saying 'Where would *you* be if you were a fire truck'?"

"Okay, where would *you* be if you were a photograph?"

"In an album," Carella said.

"You find any picture albums around?"

"Nope."

"So where *else* would you be?"

"We're looking for something maybe this big," Carella

said, curling his thumb and forefinger into a C some two inches wide. "Maybe even smaller. He could have hidden it anywhere."

"Um-huh," Brown said, and nodded. "Where?"

"Did you look in those cereal boxes in the kitchen?"

"All of them. He sure liked cornflakes."

"Maybe it *is* under the carpet," Carella said.

"Would *you* put it under the carpet?"

"No. Too much trouble checking on it."

"That's what I figure. Have to move the furniture around and pull up the whole damn rug everytime you wanted to make sure the picture was still there."

"So where *would* you be?" Carella said.

"Home asleep," Brown answered.

"Okay, where *wouldn't* you be?"

"I wouldn't be in plain sight of two cops coming to look for me."

"It sure as hell ain't in plain sight," Carella said.

"Probably right under our noses, though, and we haven't yet spotted it," Brown said. "Maybe we need a little more light on the subject." He rose from the easy chair, sighed heavily, and walked to the piano. A lamp with a brass base rested on the burled walnut top. Brown switched it on. "There," he said, "how's that?"

"The better to see you with, my dear," Carella said.

"You want to look around a little more, or shall we come back in the morning and rip up the carpet?"

"Let's give it another whirl," Carella said. He got off the piano bench, walked to the middle of the room, looked around, and said "So where the hell is it?"

"You don't think he could have rolled it up and stuck it inside a cigarette or something?" Brown asked.

"Why not? Did you check out that cigarette box?"

"I looked inside it, but I didn't slit any of the cigarettes."

"Try it," Carella said. "We may get lucky." He walked to the standing floor lamp and started to unscrew the shade.

"I've already done that," Brown said.

"Right, I'm getting punchy," Carella said. He looked down into the lamp, said, "One of the bulbs is out," and then walked across the room to where Brown was slitting cigarettes open with his thumbnail.

"Just 'cause the man's a burglar," Brown said, "that don't mean he's got to be a bulb-snatcher, too."

"Course not," Carella said. "How we doing there?"

"I may get cancer of the thumb," Brown said.

He looked up at Carella. Their eyes met, and instant recognition flashed onto both their faces at the same moment, leaping the distance between them like heat lightning.

"Yeah!" Carella said, and started moving back toward the floor lamp.

"You thinking what I'm thinking?" Brown said, following him instantly.

"Oh, you *know* it," Carella said.

There were three electric light bulbs in the lamp. Two of them were illuminated, and the third one was out. Carella reached in through the open top of the shade and unscrewed the one bulb that was not burning.

"There it is," he said. "Unplug this damn thing before we electrocute ourselves."

"Talk about a light bulb going on over a man's head," Brown said, and pulled the plug. Carella reached into the open socket with his thumb and forefinger. Neatly folded in half and then in half again, nestled into the bottom of the socket where it had been hidden by the light bulb screwed in on top of it, was the piece of the photo Krutch had promised they would find.

4

THE BUREAU of Criminal Identification was located at
Headquarters, downtown on High Street. It was open
twenty-four hours a day, its sole reason for existence
being the collection, compilation, and cataloguing of any
and all information descriptive of criminals. The I.B.
maintained a Fingerprint File, a Criminal Index File, a
Wanted File, a Degenerate File, a Parolee File, a Released Prisoner File, and Known Gamblers, Known
Rapists, Known Muggers, Known You-Name-It files. Its
Modus Operandi File alone contained more than 100,000
photographs of known criminals. And since all persons
charged with and convicted of a crime were photographed
and fingerprinted as specified by law, the file was continually growing and continually being brought up to date.
The I.B. received and classified some 206,000 sets of
prints yearly, and answered requests for more than 250,-
000 criminal records from police departments all over
the country. Arthur Brown's request for information on
Albert Weinberg was one of those. The package from the
I.B. was waiting on his desk when he got to work that
Friday morning.

As Krutch had faithfully reported, Weinberg had indeed been busted several years back. According to the
supplementary information enclosed with his yellow sheet,
he had started a fist fight in a bar, and then—for no
apparent reason—suddenly attacked a little old lady who

was sitting on a stool at the end of the bar, knocking her senseless and taking seventeen dollars and eighty-four cents from her purse. He had pleaded guilty to all charges and had served his time at Castleview Prison upstate, from which he had been released two years back. He had not been in any trouble with the law since.

Brown studied the information carefully, glanced up at the clock on the squadroom wall, and decided he had better get his ass down to the Criminal Courts Building. He told Carella where he was going, advised him that he would probably try to contact Weinberg later that day, and then left the office. He thought of the snapshot all the way downtown. There were now three pieces: the one they had found clenched in the dead Ehrbach's fist, and which was shaped somewhat like a dancing girl; the one Irving Krutch had voluntarily delivered to the squadroom, and which was obviously a corner piece; and now the one they had found hidden in Ehrbach's floor lamp, shaped like a drunken amoeba. He kept thinking of those pieces all during the trial.

His testimony was relatively simple. He explained to the assistant district attorney that at the time of the arrest, the defendant Michael Lloyd had been sitting in the kitchen of his home with a bloody bread knife in his hand. His wife was in the bedroom, stabbed in the shoulder. Her lover was no place to be found; he had apparently left in a great hurry, leaving behind his shoes and his socks. Brown testified that the defendant Michael Lloyd had not resisted arrest, and that he had told the arresting officers that he had tried to kill his wife and hoped the bitch was dead. On the basis of his statement and the evidence of the bloody knife in his hands and the wounded woman in the bedroom, he had been charged with attempted murder. In the cross-examination, the defense lawyer asked a lot of questions about Lloyd's "alleged" statement at the time of his arrest, wanting of course to know whether the prisoner had been properly advised of his rights, and Brown testified that everything had been conducted according to Miranda-Escobedo, and the district attorney excused him without a redirect, and called his next witness, the patrolman who had been p esent in the apartment when Lloyd had made his statement about having wanted to kill his wife. Brown left the Criminal Courts Building at three that afternoon.

Now, at 6 P.M., he sat at a table near the plate-glass front window of a cafeteria called The R&R, and knew

that he was being cased from the street outside by none
other than Albert Weinberg himself in person. Weinberg
was even bigger than Krutch had described him, and
certainly bigger than he had looked in the I.B.'s mug
shot. At least as tall as Brown, heavier, with tremendous
shoulders and powerful arms, a huge barrel chest and
massive hands, he walked past the plate-glass window
four times before deciding to come into the restaurant.
He was wearing a plaid, long-sleeved sports shirt, the
sleeves rolled up past his thick wrists. His reddish-blond
hair was curly and long, giving his green-eyed face a
cherubic look that denied the brute power of his body.
He came directly to Brown's table, approaching him with
the confident stride most very strong men possess, stood
staring down at him, and immediately said, "You look
like fuzz."

"So do you," Brown answered.

"How do I know you're not?"

"How do I know *you're* not?" Brown said. "Why don't
you sit down?"

"Sure," Weinberg answered. He pulled out a chair, ad-
justed his body to the seat and back as though he were
maneuvering a bulldozer into a tight corner, and then
folded his huge hands on the tabletop. "Let's hear it
again," he said.

"From the top?"

"From the top," Weinberg said, and nodded. "First,
your name."

"Artie Stokes. I'm from Salt Lake City, you ever been
there?"

"No."

"Nice city," Brown said. "Do you ski? Supposed to be
great powder skiing at Alta."

"Did you call me to talk about the Olympics, or what?"
Weinberg said.

"I thought you might be a skier," Brown answered.

"Are *you?*"

"How many Negroes have you ever seen on the ski
slopes?"

"I've never been *on* the ski slopes."

"But you get my point."

"I'm still waiting for your story, Stokes."

"I already gave it to you on the phone."

"Give it to me again."

"Why?"

"Let's say we had a poor connection."

"Okay," Brown said, and sighed. "Couple of weeks ago, I bought a piece of a picture and a couple of names from a guy in Salt Lake. I paid two grand for the package. Guy who sold it to me was fresh out of Utah State, and strapped for cash."

"What's his name?"

"Danny Firth. He was doing eight years for armed robbery, got out in April and needed a stake to set up his next job. That's why he was willing to part with what he had."

"What'd he have?"

"I just told you. Two names and a piece of a snapshot."

"And you were willing to pay two grand for *that?*"

"That's right."

"Why?"

"Because Firth told me I could get seven hundred and fifty thousand dollars just by fitting my peice of the snapshot into the whole picture."

"He told you that, huh?"

"That's what he told me."

"I'm surprised he didn't sell you the Calm's Point Bridge while he was at it."

"This ain't the Calm's Point Bridge, Weinberg, and you know it."

Weinberg was silent for a few moments. He kept looking down at his clasped hands. Then he raised his eyes to Brown's and said, "You've a piece of the snapshot, huh?"

"That's right."

"And two names, huh?"

"That's right."

"What're the two names?"

"Yours is one of them."

"And the other one?"

"I'll tell you that after we make a deal."

"And what're these names supposed to be?"

"They're supposed to be the names of two people who've *also* got pieces of that picture."

"And two names, huh?"

"That's right."

"You're nuts," Weinberg said.

"I told you most of this on the phone," Brown said. "If you think I'm nuts, what're you doing here?"

Weinberg studied him again. He unclasped his hands, took a cigarette from a package in his pocket, offered one to Brown, and then lighted both of them. He let out a stream of smoke, leaned back in his chair, and said, "Did your pal Danny Firth say *how* you could get seven hundred and fifty G's for pasting a picture together?"

"He did."

"How?"

"Weinberg . . . *you* know, and *I* know the full picture shows where Carmine Bonamico dropped the N.S.L.A. loot."

"I don't know what you're talking about."

"You know *exactly* what I'm talking about. Now how about it? You want to keep playing cute, or you want to talk a deal?"

"I want some more information."

"Like what?"

"Like how'd your pal Danny Firth come across his piece?"

"He got it from a guy at Utah State. The guy was doing life, no chance of getting out unless he *busted* out, which he wasn't about to do. Danny promised to look after his wife and kids if he recovered the loot."

"So Danny gets out, and turns right around and sells you his piece, huh?"

"That's right."

"Nice guy, Danny."

"What do you expect?" Brown said, and smiled. "Honor among thieves?"

"Which brings us to you," Weinberg said, returning the smile. "What's *your* bag?"

"I'm in and out of a lot of things."

"Like what?"

"The last thing I was in and out of was San Quentin," Brown said, and smiled again. "I did five years for hanging some paper. It was a bum rap."

"It's *always* a bum rap," Weinberg said. "Let's get back to the picture for a minute. How many pieces *are* there, do you know?"

"I was hoping you'd know."

"I don't."

"We can talk a deal, anyway."

"Maybe," Weinberg said. "Who else knows about this?"

"Nobody."

"You sure you didn't tell your brother all about it? Or some broad?"

"I haven't *got* a brother. And I never tell broads nothing." Brown paused. "Why? Who'd *you* tell?"

"Not a soul. You think I'm crazy? There's big money involved here."

"Oh, all at once you *know* there's big money involved, huh?"

"What's the other name on your list?"

"Do we have a deal?"

"Only if it's a name I don't already have."

"How many do you have?"

"Just one."

"That makes us even."

"Unless it's the same name."

"If it's the same name, neither of us have lost anything. Here's the deal, Weinberg, take it or leave it. I put up the name and the piece *I've* got, you put up the name and the piece *you've* got. If we find the loot, we split it fifty-fifty—*after* deducting expenses. I've already laid out two grand, you know."

"That's your headache," Weinberg said. "I'm willing to share whatever expenses we have from now on, but don't expect me to pay for a *bar mitzvah* when you were thirteen."

"Okay, forget the two grand. Have we got a deal?"

"We've got a deal," Weinberg said, and extended his hand across the table. Brown took it. "Let's see your piece of the picture," Weinberg said.

"Amateur night in Dixie," Brown said, shaking his head. "You didn't *really* think I'd have it with me, did you?"

"No harm trying," Weinberg said, and grinned. "Meet me later tonight. We'll put it all on the table then."

"Where?"

"My place?" Weinberg asked.

"Where's that?"

"220 South Kirby. Apartment 36."

"What time?"

"Eleven o'clock okay with you?"

"I'll be there," Brown said.

220 South Kirby was in a slum as rank as a cesspool. Arthur Brown knew such slums well. The overflowing garbage cans in front of the building were quite familiar to him. The front stoop held no surprises; cracked cement steps, the middle riser of which was lettered in white paint with the words NO SITTING ON STOOP; rusted wrought-iron railings; a shattered pane of glass in the entrance door. The locks on the mailboxes in the foyer,

where welfare checks were deposited each month, were broken. There was no light in the foyer and only a single naked bulb illuminated the first-floor landing. The hall-way smelled of cooking, breathing, eliminating. The stench that assailed Brown as he climbed to the third floor brought back too many memories of a lanky boy lying in bed in his underwear, listening to the sounds of rats foraging in the kitchen. His sister, in the bed next to his, in the same bedroom shared by his mother and father, would whisper in the darkness, "Are they here again, Artie?" and he would nod wide-eyed and say reassuringly, "They'll go away, Penny."

One night, Penny said, "Suppose they don't, Artie?"

He could find no answer. In his mind's eye, he saw himself walking into the kitchen the next morning to discover the room swarming with long-tailed rats, their sharp fangs dripping blood.

Even now, he shuddered at the thought.

Suppose they don't, Artie?

His sister had died at the age of seventeen, from an overdose of heroin administered in a cellar club by a teen-age girl who, like Penny, was one of the debs in a street gang called The Warrior Princes. He could remember a time when one of the boys painted the name of the gang in four-foot high letters on the brick wall of a housing project—THE WARIOR PRINCES.

In the darkness of the third-floor landing, Brown rapped on the door to 36, and heard Weinberg say from within, "Yes, who is it?"

"Me," he answered. "Stokes."

"It's open, come in," Weinberg said.

He opened the door.

Something warned him a second too late. As he opened the door, he could see through into the kitchen, but Weinberg was nowhere in sight. And then the warning came, the knowledge that Weinberg's voice had sounded very near to the closed door. He turned to his right, started to bring up his hand in protection against the coming blow—but too late. Something hard hit him on the side of his head, just below the temple. He fell side-ways, almost blacked out, tried to get to his knees, stumbled, and looked up into the muzzle of a .38 Special.

"Hello there, Stokes," Weinberg said, and grinned. "Keep your hands flat on the floor, don't make a move or I'll kill you. That's it."

He stepped gingerly around Brown, reached under his

jacket from behind, and pulled his gun from the shoulder holster there.

"I hope you've got a license for this," he said, grinned again, and tucked the gun into the waistband of his trousers. "Now get up."

"What do you hope to accomplish?" Brown said.

"I hope to get what I want without having to make any cockamamie deals."

"And when you've got it? Then what?"

"I move on to bigger and better things. With*out* you."

"You'd better move far and fast," Brown said. "I'm sure as hell going to find you."

"Not if you're dead, you won't."

"You'd cool me in your own apartment? Who're you trying to kid?"

"It's *not* my apartment," Weinberg said, and grinned again.

"I checked the address with . . ." Brown started, and shut his mouth before he'd said, "the Identification Bureau."

"Yeah, with what?"

"With your name in the phone book. Don't try to con me, Weinberg. This is your pad, all right."

"*Used* to be, only *used* to be. I moved out two months ago, kept the same phone number."

"Then how'd you get in here tonight?"

"The super's a wino. A bottle of Thunderbird goes a long way in this building."

"What about whoever lives here now?"

"He's a night watchman. He leaves here at ten and doesn't get home until six in the morning. Any other questions?"

"Yeah," Brown said. "What makes you think I'm in this alone?"

"What difference does it make?"

"I'll tell you what difference it makes. You can take my piece of the snapshot—oh, sure, I've got it with me—but if I *am* in this with another guy, or *two* other guys, or a *dozen* other guys, you can bet your ass they've all got prints of it. So where does that leave you? I'm dead, and you've got the picture, but so have they. You're right back where you started."

"*If* there's anybody else in it with you."

"Right. And if there's anybody else, they know who you are, pal, believe me. You pull that trigger, you'd better start running. Fast."

"You told me nobody knew about this."

"Sure. You told *me* we had a deal."

"Maybe you're full of shit this time, too."

"Or maybe not. You ready to chance it? You know the kind of heat you'd be asking for? Oh, not only from the cops—homicide's still against the law, you know. But also from . . ."

"The cops don't bother me. They'll go looking for the guy who lives here."

"Unless one of my friends tells them you and I had a meeting here tonight."

"It sounds very good, Stokes. But only if you've *really* got some friends out there. Otherwise, it ain't worth a nickel."

"Consider another angle then. You kill me, and you get my piece of the picture, sure. But you don't get that name you want. That's up *here,* Weinberg." He tapped his temple with his forefinger.

"I hadn't thought of that," Weinberg said.

"Think about it now," Brown said. "I'll give you five minutes."

"You'll give *me* five minutes?" Weinberg said, and burst out laughing. *"I'm* holding the gun, and *you're* giving me five minutes."

"Always play 'em like you've got 'em, my daddy used to tell me," Brown said, and smiled.

"Your daddy ever get hit with a slug from a .38?"

"No, but he *did* get hit with a baseball bat one time," Brown said, and Weinberg burst out laughing again.

"Maybe you wouldn't make such a bad partner after all," he said.

"So what do you think?"

"I don't know."

"Put up the gun. Give mine back, and we'll be on equal terms again. Then let's cut the crap and get on with the goddamn business."

"How do I know you won't try to cold-cock me?"

"Because maybe *you've* got friends, too, same as me."

"Always play 'em like you've got 'em," Weinberg said, and chuckled.

"Yes or no?"

"Sure," Weinberg said. He took Brown's gun from his waistband and handed it to him muzzle first. Brown immediately put it back into his holster. Weinberg hesitated a moment, and then put his own gun into a holster on his right hip. "Okay," he said. "Do we shake hands all over again?"

"I'd like to," Brown said.

The two men shook hands.

"Let's see your piece of the picture," Weinberg said.

"Let's see yours," Brown said.

"The Mutual Faith and Trust Society," Weinberg said. "Okay, we'll do it together."

Together, both men took out their wallets. Together, both men removed from plastic compartments the glossy segments of the larger photograph. The piece Brown placed on the tabletop was the one he and Carella had found hidden in Ehrbach's floor lamp. The piece Weinberg placed beside it was a corner piece unlike any the police already had in their possession.

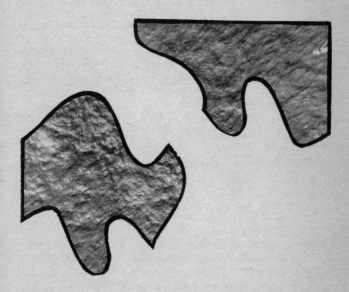

Both men studied the pieces. Weinberg began moving them around on the tabletop. A grin cracked across his face. "We're gonna make good partners," he said. "Look at this. They *fit*."

Brown looked.

Then he smiled. He smiled because the pieces sure as hell did fit. But he also smiled because, heh-heh, unbeknownst to his new partner and straight man, there were

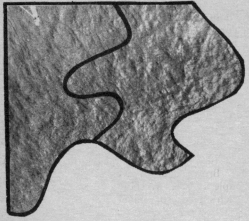

two additional pieces of the picture in the top drawer of his desk back at the squadroom, and two and two make four, and who knew what *these* two pieces and *those* two pieces together might reveal, who indeed? So Brown smiled and Weinberg smiled, and everybody was having just a wonderful old time putting together the pieces of this old jigsaw puzzle.

"Now the names," Weinberg said, sounding very much like the M.C. at the Annual Academy Awards Presentations.

"Eugene Edward Ehrbach," Brown said, smiling.

"Geraldine Ferguson," Weinberg said, smiling.

"Ehrbach's dead," Brown said, and the smile dropped from Weinberg's face.

"What?" he shouted. "What the hell kind of . . .?"

"He was killed Wednesday night. The cops found . . ."

"Dead?" Weinberg shouted. *"Dead?"*

"Dead," Brown said. "But the cops found . . ."

"Is this a double cross? Is that what this is? Some kind of a double cross?"

"You've got to learn to calm down," Brown said.

"I'll calm down! I'll break your head in a million pieces, that's what I'll do."

"He was carrying a piece of the picture," Brown said softly.

"What? Who?"

"Ehrbach."

"A piece of *our* picture?"

"That's right."

"Why didn't you say so? Where is it?"

"The cops have it."

"The cops! Jesus Christ, Stokes . . ."

"Cops can be bought," Brown said, "same as anybody else. Ehrbach's dead and anything they found on him is probably in a brown paper bag someplace being watched by a police clerk. All we got to do is find out where, and then cross a few palms."

"I don't like negotiating with fuzz," Weinberg said.

"Who does? But to survive in this city, you *got* to deal with them every now and then."

"Biggest fuckin' thieves in the world," Weinberg said.

"Look," Brown said, "if even a felony can be squared for a couple of bills, we should be able to lay our hands on Ehrbach's piece for maybe fifty, sixty bucks. All we got to do is find out where it is."

"How do we do that? Call the cops and ask?"

"Maybe. I got to think about it a little. Now what about this Geraldine what's-her-name?"

"Ferguson. She runs an art gallery on Jefferson Avenue. I've busted into her apartment maybe six or seven times already, couldn't find the picture. I wouldn't be surprised she stuck it up her twat," Weinberg said, and burst out laughing. Brown laughed with him. They were still good old buddies and still thrilled and amazed by the fact that their two separate pieces fit together as neatly as Yin and Yang.

"Have you got a print of this?" Brown asked.

"Naturally," Weinberg said. "And you?"

"Naturally."

"You want to exchange pieces, is that it?"

"That's it."

"Done," Weinberg said, and picked up the section Brown had placed on the tabletop. Brown picked up the remaining section, and both men grinned again. "Now let's go down for a drink," Weinberg said. "We got a lot of strategy to work out."

"Right," Brown said. As they went toward the front door, he said—casually, he thought—"By the way, how'd you happen to *get* your piece of the snapshot?"

"Be happy to tell you," Weinberg said.

"Good."

"As soon as you tell me how you *really* got yours," Weinberg added, and began chuckling.

Brown suddenly wondered which of them was the straight man.

5

It was all happening too quickly and too easily.

If getting seven hundred and fifty thousand dollars was always this simple, Brown was definitely in the wrong racket. He almost wished that he and Weinberg were truly partners. There was something about the big man that Brown liked, despite the fact that he was a felon. He did not leave Weinberg until two o'clock the next morning. By that time, each of the men had consumed a fifth of Scotch between them, and were calling each other Artie and Al. They had also decided that Brown should be the one who made the next approach to Geraldine Ferguson. Weinberg had been to her gallery several times with offers to buy the segment he was certain she possessed, but each time she had professed ignorance of the photograph, segmented or otherwise. Weinberg told Brown that he *knew* the girl had the goods they were after, but he would not reveal *how* he knew. Brown said that was a hell of a way to start a partnership, and Weinberg said Brown had started in an even *worse* way, giving him all that bullshit about a lifer at Utah State, man, that was straight out of Mickey Mouse, had Brown expected him to believe it? Brown said Well, I guess we both got our reasons for not wanting our sources known, and Weinberg said Well, maybe when we get to know each other better, and Brown said I hope so, and Weinberg said Man, I never thought I'd be partners with a spade.

Brown looked at him.

It was hip these days, he knew, for white men to call Negroes "spades," but to Brown this was simply another of the words which had once been considered—and which he *still* considered—derogatory. Weinberg was smiling in a boozy happy friendly way, and Brown was certain the slur had been unintentional. And yet, the word rankled, the whole fucking thing rankled.

"That bother you?" he asked.

"What bother me?" Weinberg said.

"My being a *spade*," Brown said, hitting the word hard.

Weinberg looked him square in the eye. "Did I say that? Did I call you that?"

"You did," Brown said, and nodded.

"Then I'm sorry. I didn't mean it." He extended his hand across the table. "I'm sorry, Artie," he said.

Brown took his hand. "Forget it."

"I may be a shit," Weinberg said. "I may go around beating up people and doing rotten things, but I like you, Artie, and I wouldn't hurt you by saying no dumb thing like that."

"Okay."

Weinberg was just gathering steam. "I may be the crumbiest guy ever walked the earth, I may have done some filthy things, but one thing I wouldn't do is call you no spade, Artie, not if I wasn't so piss-ass drunk and didn't know what I was saying that might hurt a good friend of mine and a partner besides."

"Okay," Brown said.

"Okay, excuse it, Artie. Excuse it. I mean it."

"Okay."

"Okay," Weinberg said. "Let's go home, Artie. Artie, I think we better go home. I always get in fights in bars, and I don't want to get in no trouble when we got our little deal cooking, okay?" He winked. "Okay?" He winked again. "Tomorrow morning, you got to go visit little Geraldine Ferguson. Tell her she don't give us that picture, we'll come around and do something terrible to her, okay?" Weinberg smiled. "I can't think of nothing terrible right now, but I'll think of something in the morning, okay?"

On Saturday morning, Brown put the new photo scrap into an envelope together with Geraldine Ferguson's name and address, sealed the envelope, and dropped it into a mailbox in the hallway of 1134 Culver Avenue, three blocks from the precinct. The name on the box was Cara Binieri, which was Steve Carella's little joke, *carabinieri* meaning fuzz in Italian. They had decided between them that Brown was to stay away from the squadroom, and whereas he hoped to call Carella later in the day, he wanted the information to be waiting for him in the mailbox this morning, when he would pick it up on his way to work.

Brown's own day started somewhat more glamorously. It also ended in a pretty glamorous way.

Geraldine Ferguson was a white woman, petite, with long straight black hair and brown eyes and a generous mouth. She was in her early thirties, wearing purple bell-bottom slacks and a man-tailored shirt done in lavender satin. She had big golden hoops looped into her ear lobes, and she greeted Brown with a smile nothing less than radiant.

"Good morning," she said. "Isn't it a *beautiful* morning?"

"It's a lovely morning," Brown said.

"Are you here for the Gonzagos?" she asked.

"I don't think so," Brown said. "What *are* the gonzagos?"

"Luis Gonzago," she said, and smiled again. "He's a painter. I thought you might have wanted to see his stuff, but we've already taken it down. Will you be going to Los Angeles?"

"No, I hadn't planned to," Brown said.

"Because he'll be having a show at the Herron Gallery out there starting next Tuesday. On Sepulveda."

"No, I won't be going to Los Angeles."

"That's a shame," she said, and smiled.

She was perhaps five-two or five-three, with a perfectly proportioned figure for her size. She moved with a swift feminine grace that he found delightful, her brown eyes flashing in the sunlight that streamed through the front plate-glass window, the smile breaking as sharp and as fast as a curve ball. She threw her arms wide, and said, "But we've got loads of other stuff, so if you'd like me to help you, I'd be happy to. Or you can just look around on your own, if you like. What were you interested in? Paintings or sculpture?"

"Well," Brown said, and hesitated, wondering exactly

how he should play this. "Is this your own gallery?" he asked, stalling.

"Yes, it is," she said.

"Then you're Miss Ferguson. I mean, this *is* the Ferguson Gallery, so I guess . . ."

"Well, *Mrs.* Ferguson, really," she said. "But *not* really," she added, and the smile broke again, swift and clean. "I was married to Mr. Ferguson, Mr. *Harold* Ferguson, but Mr. Ferguson and I are no longer sharing bed and board, and so whereas I'm still Geraldine Ferguson, I am no longer *Mrs.* Ferguson. Oh hell," she said, "why don't you just call me Gerry? What's *your* name?"

"Arthur Stokes," he said.

"Are you a cop, Arthur?" she asked flatly.

"No," he said. "What gave you that idea?"

"You're big like a cop," she said, and shrugged. "Also, you carry a gun."

"Do I?"

"Mm-huh. Right there," she said, and pointed.

"I didn't think it showed."

"Well, Harold was in the diamond business, and he had a carry-permit, and he used to wear this *enormous* revolver in a shoulder holster, right where yours is. So I guess when your husband wears a gun all the time, you get used to the way it looks, and that's how I spotted yours right away. Why do you wear a gun, Arthur? Are you in the diamond business?"

"No," he said, "I'm in the insurance business."

He figured that was a fair enough beginning, even though he had borrowed the occupation from Irving Krutch who, to his knowledge, did *not* carry a gun.

"Oh, do insurance men wear guns?" Gerry asked. "I didn't know that."

"Yes," he said, "if they're insurance investigators."

"Don't *tell* me!" she squealed. "Someone's had a painting stolen! You're here to check on authenticity."

"Well, no," he said. "Not exactly."

"Arthur," she said, "I think you're a cop, I really do."

"Now why would a cop be visiting *you,* Miss Ferguson?"

"Gerry. Maybe because I charge such exorbitant prices," she said, and smiled. "I don't really. Yes, I do really. Would you like to see some pictures while you decide if you're a cop or not?"

She led him around the gallery. The walls were white, with recessed overhead lighting fixtures that illuminated the hanging paintings and standing pieces of sculpture. Her taste in paintings was a bit far-out for Brown, wildly colorful, non-objective geometric tangles that overpowered the eye and defied analysis. The sculpture was of the junkyard variety, automobile headlights welded to Stillson wrenches, a plumber's red-cupped plunger wired to the broken handle and frayed-straw brush of a broom.

"I can see we're hardly eliciting any wild response," Gerry said, and smiled. "What kind of art do you like?"

"Well, I did have a specific picture in mind," Brown said.

"Did someone see it here?" she asked. "Would it have been in the Gonzago exhibit?"

"I don't think so."

"What kind of a painting is it?"

"It isn't a painting. It's a photograph."

Gerry shook her head. "It couldn't have been here. We've never had a photographic show, not since I've owned the gallery, anyway—and that's close to five years."

"It's not even a *whole* photograph," Brown said, and watched her.

"Oh-*ho*," she said. This time, she didn't smile. "What happened to the other guy?"

"What other guy?"

"The guy who's been in here three or four thousand times in the past two months. He's *yay* tall, and he's got blondish curly hair, and he said his name was Al Reynolds the first time he came in, and then forgot what he'd told me and said his name was Al *Randolph* the second time around. Is *he* a cop, too?"

"We're neither of us cops."

"Mr. Stark . . ."

"Stokes," Brown said.

"Just checking," Gerry said, and grinned. "Mr. Stokes . . ."

"Arthur . . ."

"Arthur, I don't have what you're looking for. Believe me. If I had it, I'd sell it to you. Assuming the price was right."

"The price can be made right."

"How right is right?"

"You name a figure," Brown said.

"Well, do you see that Albright on the wall there? It's approximately four feet square, and the gallery gets ten thousand dollars for it. The smaller painting next to it, the Sandrovich, costs five thousand. And the tiny *gouache* on the far wall costs three thousand. How large is your photograph, Arthur?"

"I have no idea. Are we talking about the *whole* picture now, or just the piece you have?"

"The whole picture."

"Five by seven? Six by eight? I'm guessing."

"Then you've never seen the whole picture?"

"Have you?"

"I haven't even seen the tiny piece you're after."

"Then how do you know it's tiny?" Brown asked.

"How much is it worth to you and your friend, Arthur? Tiny or otherwise?"

"Have you got it?"

"If I told him no, why should I tell you yes?"

"Maybe I'm more persuasive."

"Sure, look at Superspade," Gerry said, and smiled. "Faster than a rolling watermelon, able to leap tall honkies in a single bound . . ."

". . . who is in reality," Brown continued, "mild-mannered Arthur Stokes of *Ebony* magazine."

"Who are you *really* in reality, Arthur?"

"An insurance investigator, I told you."

"Your friend Reynolds or Randolph or whoever-the-hell doesn't look or sound like an insurance investigator."

"No two insurance investigators look or sound alike."

"That's right. Only cops and crooks look and sound alike. Are you and your friend cops, Arthur? Or crooks? Which?"

"Maybe one of us is a cop and the other's a crook."

"Either way, I don't have what you want."

"I think you have."

"You're right," a voice said from the rear of the gallery. "She has."

"Oh, hell," Gerry said.

Brown turned to where a blue door had opened in the otherwise white wall. A blond man in a brown suit stood in the open doorway, his hand still on the knob. He was about five feet ten inches tall, wearing a vest under the suit jacket, gold-rimmed eyeglasses, a brown-and-gold striped tie. He walked briskly to where they were standing, offered his hand to Brown and said, "Bramley Kahn, how do you do?"

"Bram, you're a pain in the ass," Gerry said.

"Arthur Stokes," Brown said. "Pleased to meet you."

"If we're going to talk business . . ."

"We are *not* going to talk business," Gerry interrupted.

"I suggest," Kahn continued in his mild voice, "that we go into the office." He paused, glanced at Gerry, looked back at Brown, and said, "Shall we?"

"Why not?" Brown said.

They walked to the rear of the gallery. The office was small and simply decorated—a Danish modern desk, a single naturalistic painting of a nude on the wall opposite the desk, a thick gray rug, white walls, a white Lucite hanging light globe, several leather-and-chrome easy chairs. Gerry Ferguson, pouting, sat nearest Kahn's desk, folding her legs up under her and cupping her chin in her hand. Brown took the seat opposite Kahn, who sat behind the desk in an old-fashioned swivel chair that seemed distinctly out of place in such svelte surroundings.

"I'm Gerry's partner," Kahn explained.

"Only in the *gallery*," Gerry snapped.

"I'm also her business adviser."

"I've got some advice for *you*," Gerry said heatedly. "Keep you nose . . ."

"Gerry has a temper," Kahn said.

"Gerry has a jerk for a partner," Gerry said.

"Oh, my," Kahn said, and sighed.

Brown watched him, trying to determine whether he was a fag or not. His manner was effete, but not quite feminine; his voice was gently modulated, but there was no evidence in it of characteristic homosexual cadences; his gestures were small and fluid, but he neither dangled a limp wrist, nor used his hands and shoulders like a dancer's. Brown couldn't tell. The biggest queen he'd ever known had been built like a wrestler and moved with all the subtle grace of a longshoreman.

"What about the picture?" Brown asked.

"She has it," Kahn said.

"I *haven't*," Gerry said.

"Maybe I ought to leave you two alone for a while," Brown said.

"How much are you willing to pay for it, Mr. Stokes?" Kahn asked.

"That depends."

"On what?"

Brown said nothing.

Kahn said, "On whether or not it's a piece you already have, isn't that the answer?"

Brown still said nothing.

"You *do* have a piece, don't you? Or *several* pieces?"

"Is it for sale or not?" Brown asked.

"No," Gerry said.

"Yes," Kahn said. "But you still haven't made an offer, Mr. Stokes."

"Let me see it first," Brown said.

"No," Kahn said.

"No," Gerry said, just a beat behind him.

"How many pieces do you have, Mr. Stokes?"

No answer.

"Is the other gentleman your partner? Do you have more than one piece?"

No answer.

"Do you know what the picture is supposed to reveal?"

"Let *me* ask a few," Brown said.

"Please," Kahn said, and offered him the floor with an open-handed, palm-up gesture.

"Miss Ferguson . . ."

"I thought it was Gerry."

"Gerry . . . where did you get the piece you now have?"

"You're both dreaming," Gerry said. "I don't know what either one of you is talking about."

"My client . . ."

"Your client, my ass," Gerry said. "You're a cop. Who are you trying to kid, Arthur?"

"Are you a policeman, Mr. Stokes?"

"No."

"The fuzz stench is overpowering," Gerry said.

"How do you come to be so familiar with that stench?" Brown asked.

"May I answer that one?" Kahn asked.

"Keep your mouth shut, Bram," Gerry warned.

"Mrs. Ferguson's sister is a girl named Patty D'Amore," Kahn said. "Does that mean anything to you?"

"Not a thing," Brown said.

"Her husband was a cheap gangster named Louis D'Amore. He was killed some six years ago, following a bank holdup."

"I don't keep track of such things," Brown said.

"No, I'll just *bet* you don't," Gerry said. "He's a cop, Bram. And *you're* a fool."

"Sicilian blood is much, *much* thicker than water," Kahn said, and smiled. "I would imagine that in your childhood, there was plenty of talk concerning the 'stench of fuzz' while the lasagna was being served, eh, Geraldine?"

"How would you like to hear a choice Sicilian expression?" Gerry asked.

"I'd love to."

"Va fon gool," Gerry said.

"Even *I* know what that means," Brown said.

"Sounds Chinese," Kahn said.

"About the picture . . ."

"We have it, and we'll sell it," Kahn said. "That's our business. Selling pictures."

"Have you got any customers who'll buy a picture sight unseen?" Brown asked.

"Have we got any customers who'll buy a picture that doesn't even exist?" Gerry asked.

"Well," Brown said, "why don't you give me a ring when you've settled this between you, huh?"

"Where can we reach you, Mr. Stokes?"

"I'm staying at the Selby Arms. It's a fleabag on North Founders, just off Byram Lane."

"Are you an out-of-towner, Mr. Stokes?"

"Room 502," Brown said.

"You didn't answer my question."

"You didn't answer any of mine, either," Brown said. He smiled, rose, turned to Gerry and said, "I hope you'll reconsider, Miss Ferguson."

This time, she didn't ask him to call her Gerry.

On the street outside, Brown looked for a phone booth. The first phone he tried had the dial missing. The receiver on the next phone had been severed from its metal-covered cord, undoubtedly with a wire cutter. The third booth he found seemed okay. He put a dime into the phone and got nothing, no dial tone, no static, no nothing. He jiggled the hook. His dime did not come back. He hung up the receiver. His dime did not come back. He hit the phone with his fist. Nothing. He went out of the booth swearing, wondering when the city was going to crack down on the illegal gambling devices the telephone company had installed all over the city and labeled "Public Telephones." He supposed a Gaylord Ravenal type would have enjoyed this kind of action—you put your money in the slot and either lost it, or else hit the jackpot and a shower of coins came out of the return chute—but Brown merely wanted to make a telephone call, and the Las Vegas aspects of such an endeavor left him absolutely cold. He finally found a working telephone in a restaurant off Tyler. With a glance heavenward, he put his dime into the slot. He got a dial tone immediately.

The number he dialed was Albert Weinberg's. Weinberg had given him his new address the night before, a
rooming house on North Colman, close to Byram Lane,
which was why Brown had checked into the Selby Arms,
only three blocks away from Weinberg's place. When
Weinberg came onto the line, Brown related his encoun-
ter with the owners of the Ferguson Gallery and said
he hoped to hear from them later in the day, was in
fact heading back to the hotel right this minute.

"That's the Selby Arms, right?" Weinberg said.

"Yeah, on North Founders. How'd *you* make out?"

"I've been doing a little asking around," Weinberg
said, "and the way I understand it, whenever some guy's
been knocked off, the cops take his clothes and his be-
longings downtown to what they call the Property Clerk's
Office. The stuff can be claimed by a relative after the
medics, and the lab, and the bulls on the case are finished
with it. You think I could pass for Ehrbach's brother?"

"*I* sure as hell couldn't," Brown said.

"Might be worth a try, save ourselves a few bucks."

"A fix is safer," Brown said.

"Let me go on the earie a bit longer," Weinberg said,
"try to find out who runs that office."

"Okay. You know where to reach me."

"Right. Let me know if Ferguson or her pansy partner get in touch."

"I will," Brown said, and hung up.

In the cloistered stillness of the squadroom (telephones jangling, typewriters clanging, teletype clattering,
a prisoner screaming his head off in the detention cage
across the room), Steve Carella spread the four pieces
of the photograph on his desktop and tried to fit them
together.

He was not very good at working jigsaw puzzles.

The way he looked at it, and there were *many* ways of
looking at it, the right-angle pieces were obviously corner
pieces, which meant that either of them could go in any
one of four places, most rectangles having four and only
four corners, brilliant deduction. The simplest of these
two corner pieces looked like nothing more than a dark
rough surface with something jutting into it from above
or below, depending on whether the corner was a top
corner or a bottom corner. The something jutting into
the dark rough surface strongly resembled a phallus
with a string around it. (He doubted very much that it

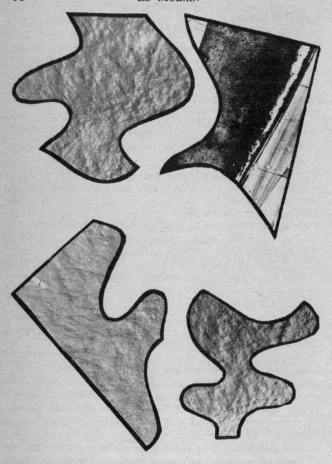

was actually a phallus. If it was, they had an entirely
different kind of case on their hands.) The second corner
piece, the one with the sweeping curves, seemed to be a
section of a wall or a building or a handball court. Which
brought him to the two remaining pieces, both with the
same rough gray surface. It was the surface that trou-
bled Carella. The more he looked at it, the more it looked
like water—but how could that tie in with the wall or
building or handball court in the corner piece?

He was not very good at working jigsaw puzzles.

After ten minutes of study, he finally managed to fit two of the pieces together, a task Albert Weinberg had completed in thirty seconds. Ten minutes later, he had fitted another piece into the puzzle. Twenty minutes after that, he was convinced that the fourth piece did not fit against any of the other three. He looked at what he now had:

It could have been anything, anywhere.

In the city June worked its balmy Saturday afternoon magic.

On Third and Folger, two seventeen-year-old boys stopped a younger boy and asked him if he had any money. This being Saturday, the younger boy had no school carfare, and no lunch money. All he had was an overriding fear that transmitted itself to the older boys like animal musk in a virgin forest. When they discovered he was broke, they beat him up. It is probable that all they wanted to do was beat him up in the first place. They left him senseless, his nose shattered, four teeth knocked out of his mouth. All they took from him was a Ban-the-Bomb button he was wearing on his jacket. Then they went to a movie where John Wayne was starring in *The Green Berets.*

June.

In Grover Park, an old lady sat on a bench feeding the

pigeons. She was wearing a flowered housedress and a woolen shawl. She kept feeding the pigeons and cooing to them gently. Her bag was on the bench beside her. From its open top, a half-completed gray sweater and a pair of knitting needles protruded. A college student with long hair and a straggly beard ambled over, and sat on the bench beside her. He was wearing blue jeans and a sweat shirt and scuffed desert boots. He opened a copy of Plato's *Republic* and began reading in the sunshine.

The old lady glanced at him.

She threw a handful of bread crumbs to the pigeons, cooed at them, and glanced again at the boy, who was absorbed in his book.

"Don't you look at *me* that way," she said suddenly.

The boy looked sharply to his right, not sure at first that he was being addressed.

"You heard me, you little shit," the old lady said. "Don't look at *me* that way, you bastard."

The boy stared at the woman for a moment, decided she was crazy, closed his book, and was rising from the bench when she reached into her bag, pulled out one of the knitting needles and stuck it clear through his eye to the back of his neck. At her feet, the pigeons pecked at the bread crumbs and gently cooed.

June, croon.

On a rooftop several miles away, the sunshine beat down on tar already growing sticky, and four boys held the twelve-year-old girl down against the black melting stuff while a fifth boy pulled off her panties and stuffed them into her mouth so that she could not scream. The girl could not move either, because they had her spread-eagled, arms and legs wide. A boy standing near the closed door of the roof whispered, "Hurry it up, Doc," and the boy named Doc, the one who had taken off her panties and who now stood over her, tall and large against the blinding sun, unzipped his fly, displayed his masculinity to her terror-ridden eyes, and then plunged himself deep inside her, against the protest of her tearing flesh. The boy standing near the closed door danced an impatient little jig while they took turns with the little girl. By the time it was his turn, they decided they'd better get out of there before somebody caught them. The little girl, bleeding and unconscious, still lay spread-eagled against the melting tar, her panties in her mouth. The boy who had been lookout complained all the way down the stairs to the street. "You bastards," he kept saying, "you promised I'd get some, too, you promised, you promised."

June, croon, spoon.

As the afternoon waned, a sweet intoxicating breeze blew in off the River Harb and insinuated itself through the narrow canyons of the city. Dusk was upon the horizon now, the sounds of the day were beginning to blend with the sounds of approaching night. The sky to the west turned blood-red and then swam the color spectrum through purple to blue to black. A thin sliver of moon curled against the stars like a pale lemon rind. In an apartment on a side street not far from the river, a man sat in undershirt and trousers, watching television. His wife, wearing a half-slip and a brassiere padded in from the kitchen carrying two open bottles of beer and two glasses. She put one beer and one glass down in front of the man, and then poured the other beer into a glass for herself. The crescent moon shone palely through the open back-yard window. The woman looked at the television screen and said, *"That* again?"

"Yeah," the man said, and picked up his bottle of beer.

"I hate that show," his wife said.

"I like it," he said.

Without a word, the woman went to the set, and turned the channel selector. Without a word, her husband got out of his chair, walked up to her swiftly and hit her eleven times with his beer bottle, twice while she was standing, twice as she slumped to the floor, and another seven times after she was unconscious and bleeding. He turned the television set back to the channel he'd been watching, and he did not call the police until the show was over, forty-five minutes later.

June, croon, spoon, moon.

In a hotel room at the Selby Arms, sixteen blocks to the west, Arthur Brown made three telephone calls in succession, and then sat back to wait for contact from Ferguson and/or Kahn. The first call he made was to his wife Caroline who deplored the fact that they'd had to cancel a dinner date, and then went on to tell Brown that she missed him and that their daughter Connie was coming down with a cold. Brown told his wife he missed her also, to which she replied, "So why don't you come home and do something about it?"

"Duty calls," he said.

"Foo," she answered.

They hung up billing and cooing and humming June,

croon, spoon, moon songs.

Brown opened his notebook to the page on which he had jotted Weinberg's address and telephone number. Weinberg answered on the third ring. As soon as they had exchanged hellos, Weinberg said, "Anything?"

"Not yet."

"You think they'll try to reach you?"

"I'm still hoping."

"I ain't had much luck, either," Weinberg said. "You know that Property Clerk's Office I was telling you about?"

"Yeah?"

"First of all, there must be forty or fifty guys working there, most of them civilians. They get crap from all over the city, anything that's been involved in accidents or crimes, anything not claimed at station houses—it's like a regular goddamn warehouse down there."

"No kidding," Brown said, as if he didn't already know.

"Yeah. There's also *cops* working there, because naturally they got a lot of weapons in the place, you dig?"

"Um-huh."

"In order to claim anything after they're done with it, you got to be a *prime* relative. It don't matter if you're a third cousin, so long as you're the closest living relative, you dig?"

"That sounds good for us," Brown said. "You could easily pass yourself off as . . ."

"Wait a second. You got to get a release from the D.A. first. You got to go to the D.A.'s *office* and get a goddamn *release*."

"That's bad," Brown said.

"That stinks," Weinberg said.

"Who runs the whole show down there?"

"I don't know yet."

"Try to find out. He's the man we've got to reach." Brown paused. "Unless you'd like to try breaking in some night."

"Ha!" Weinberg said. "Call me later, will you? Let me know if anything happens."

"Will you be there all night?"

"All night. I got a sweet bottle of bourbon, and I intend to kill it."

"Don't let it kill *you*," Brown said, and hung up.

The next person he called was Irving Krutch.

"Well, well," Krutch said, "this is a pleasant surprise."

"We've decided to make the investigation," Brown said.

"I thought you would," Krutch answered. "You found what you were looking for in Ehrbach's apartment, didn't you?"

"Yes. But even better than that."

"What do you mean?"

"We made contact with Weinberg. He has another piece of the picture, and he gave me a copy of it."

"That's *marvelous!*" Krutch said. "When can I have a look?"

"Not tonight. Can you drop by the squadroom tomorrow morning?"

"The squadroom?"

"Yes. Why? What's wrong with the squadroom?"

"Nothing. I just forgot for a minute that you guys work on Sunday."

"Ten o'clock or thereabouts," Brown said. "I won't be there, but Carella can show you the stuff."

"Fine," Krutch said. "Where can I reach *you* if I need you?"

"I'm at the Selby Arms, room 502."

"I'll jot that down, just in case." There was a pause on the line. "Selby Arms." Krutch repeated, obviously writing, "room 502, fine. Well," he said, "we're certainly off to a good start. I can't tell you how much I appreciate this."

"We all stand to gain," Brown said. "I've got to get off the phone. I'm expecting a call."

"Oh? Another lead?"

"Yes. The 'Geraldine' on your list is a Geraldine Ferguson, sister-in-law of the late Louis D'Amore. She runs an art gallery on Jefferson Avenue."

"Who gave you that?"

"Weinberg."

"Has she got anything?"

"I think so, but I'm not sure. That's what I'm waiting to hear."

"Will you let me know?"

"As soon as anything jells."

"Good. Listen, thanks again for calling. This is great news, really."

"Right, so long," Brown said, and hung up.

His telephone did not ring that night, nor did Saturday end glamorously for him until close to midnight. He had dozed in the armchair near the telephone when a knock sounded at the door. He was instantly awake.

"Yes?" he said.

"Mr. Stokes?"

"Yes."

"Desk clerk. Woman just delivered a message for you downstairs."

"Just a second," he answered. He had taken off his shoes and socks, and he padded to the door now in his bare feet and opened it just a crack.

The door flew wide, and the glamorous part of Saturday night began.

The man was wearing a glamorous nylon stocking pulled up over his face, flattening his nose, distorting his features. He was holding a glamorous pistol in his gloved right hand and as he shoved the door open with his left shoulder, he swung the gun at Brown's head, hitting him over the eye and knocking him to the floor. The man was wearing glamorous, highly polished black shoes, and he kicked Brown in the head the moment he was down. A glamorous shower of rockets went off inside Brown's skull, and then he went unconscious.

6

IT IS BAD to get hit on the head, any doctor can tell you that. It is even worse to get kicked in the head after you have been hit on the head, even your *mother* can tell you that. If a person gets hit on the head and loses consciousness, the doctors examining him will usually insist that he remain in the hospital for a period of at least one week, since unconsciousness precludes concussion, and concussion *can* mean internal hemorrhaging.

Brown regained consciousness twenty minutes later, and went into the bathroom to vomit. The room was a mess. Whoever had creamed him had also shaken down the place as thoroughly as the late Eugene Edward Ehrbach had shaken down the apartment of the late Donald Renninger. Brown was not too terribly concerned with the wreckage, not at the moment. Brown was concerned with staggering to the telephone, which he managed, and lifting the receiver, which he also managed. He gave the desk clerk Steve Carella's home number in Riverhead, waited while the phone rang six times, and then spoke to Fanny, the Carella housekeeper, who advised him that Mr. Carella was in Isola with his wife and was not expected home until one o'clock or thereabouts. He left a message for Carella to call him at the Selby Arms, hung up, thought he had better contact the squad immediately, and was trying to get the desk clerk again when a wave of dizziness washed over him. He stumbled over to the bed, threw himself full-length upon it, and closed his eyes. In a little while, he went into the bathroom to throw up a second time. When he got back to the bed, he closed his eyes and was either asleep or unconscious again within the next minute.

The morning hours of the night were beginning.

Steve Carella reached him a half-hour later. He knocked on the door to room 502, got no answer, and opened it immediately with a skeleton key. He picked his way through the debris on the floor, went directly to the bed where Brown lay unconscious on the slashed and mutilated mattress, saw the swollen lump over his partner's eye, said, "Artie?", received no reply, and went directly to the telephone. He was waiting for the desk clerk to answer the switchboard when Brown mumbled, "I'm okay."

"Like hell you are," Carella said, and jiggled the receiver-rest impatiently.

"Cool it, Steve. I'm okay."

Carella replaced the receiver, went back to the bed, and sat on the edge of it. "I want to get a meat wagon over here," he said.

"And put me out of action for a week, huh?"

"You're growing another head the size of your first one," Carella said.

"I hate hospitals," Brown said.

"How do you like comas?" Carella asked.

"I'm not in coma. Do I look like I'm in coma?"

"Let me get some ice for that lump. Jesus, that's some lump."

"The man hit me with a truck," Brown said.

Carella was jiggling the receiver-rest again. When the desk clerk came on, he said, "I didn't wake you, did I?"

"What?" the desk clerk said.

'Get some ice up here on the double. Room 502."

"Room service is closed," the desk clerk said.

"Open it. This is the police."

"Right away," the desk clerk said, and hung up.

"Some people sure pick ratty dumps to stay in," Carella said.

"Some people try to lend credence to their cover," Brown said, and attempted a smile. It didn't work. He winced in pain, and closed his eyes again.

"Did you see who did it?" Carella asked.

"I saw him, but he had a stocking over his face."

Carella shook his head. "Ever since the first movie

where a guy had a stocking over his face, we get nothing but guys with stockings over their faces." He looked around the room. "Did a nice job on the room, too."

"Beautiful," Brown said.

"We're lucky he left you alive."

"Why wouldn't he? He wasn't after me, he was after the picture."

"Who do you think it was, Artie?"

"My partner," Brown said. "Albert Weinberg."

A knock sounded on the door. Carella went to answer it. The desk clerk was standing there in his shirt sleeves, a soup dish full of ice cubes in his hands. "I had to go to the restaurant up the block for these," he complained.

"Great, thanks a lot," Carella said.

The desk clerk kept standing there. Carella reached into his pocket and handed him a quarter.

"Thanks," the desk clerk said sourly.

Carella closed the door, went into the bathroom, wrapped a towel around the ice cubes and then went back to Brown. "Here," he said, "put this on that lump."

Brown nodded, accepted the ice pack, pressed it to his swollen eye, and winced again.

"How do you know it was Weinberg?"

"I don't, for sure."

"Was he a big guy?"

"They all look big when they're about to hit you," Brown said.

"What I mean is did you get a good look at him?"

"No, it all happened . . ."

". . . in a split second," Carella said, and both men smiled. Brown winced again. "So what makes you think it was Weinberg?"

"I had him on the phone tonight," Brown said. "Told him we'd scored."

"Who else did you talk to?"

"Irving Krutch."

"So it could have been Krutch."

"Sure. It also could have been my wife Caroline. I talked to her, too."

"She pretty good with a blunt instrument?"

"As good as most," Brown said.

"How's that eye feel?"

"Terrible."

"I think I'd *better* get a meat wagon."

"No, you don't," Brown said. "We've got work to do."

"You're not the only cop in this city," Carella said.

"I'm the only one who got clobbered in this room to-night," Brown said.

Carella sighed. "One consolation, anyway," he said.

"What's that?"

"He didn't get what he came after. *That's* in my desk drawer, back at the ranch."

It was decided over Brown's protests (actually Brown only did the protesting; Carella did all the deciding) that he would be taken to Saint Catherine's Hospital a dozen blocks away, for examination and treatment in the Emergency Room. Carella left him there at 2 A.M., still grumbling, and caught a taxi over to Weinberg's apartment on North Colman. At that hour of the morning, the neighborhood resembled a lunar landscape. Weinberg's rooming house was the only building on the street that had not already been abandoned by its owners, those entrepreneurs having decided the buildings were too expensive to maintain in accordance with the city's laws; those respectable businessmen also having discovered that no one was willing to buy such white elephants; those wheeler-dealers having merely pulled out, leaving a row of run-down tenements as a gift to the city, lucky city.

There was a time, and this not too long ago, when hippies and runaways had moved into these buildings en masse, painting their colorful flower designs on the brick fronts, sleeping on mattresses spread wall-to-wall, puffing pot, dropping acid, living the happy carefree life of the commune-dweller. The regular residents of this run-down slum area, forced to live here because of certain language and racial barriers the city raised against some of its citizens, could not understand why anyone would come to live here of his own free will and choice —but they certainly knew pigeons when they saw them. The hippies, the runaways, the carefree happy commune-dwellers had no need for telephones, being in touch as they were with nature. The only time they might have needed Mr. Bell's invention was when the restless natives of the ghetto came piling into the apartment to beat up the boys and rape the girls and take whatever meager possessions were worth hocking. The hippies and the runaways decided that perhaps this wasteland was not for them, it becoming more and more difficult to repeat the word "Love" when a fist was being crashed into the mouth or a girl was screaming on the mattress in the other room. The ghetto regulars had struck back at a society that forced them to live in such surroundings, little realizing that the people they were harassing had themselves broken with the same society, a society that *allowed* such ghettos to exist. It was a case of poor slob beating up on poor slob, while five blocks away, a fashionable discotheque called Rembrandt's bleated its rock-and-roll music, and ladies in sequined slacks and men in dancing slippers laughed away the night. The hippies were gone now, the flower designs on the building fronts faded by the sun or washed away by the rain. The slum dwellers had reclaimed their disputed turf, and now their only enemies were the rats that roamed in the deserted tenement shells.

Weinberg lived in a rooming house on a street that looked as if it had suffered a nuclear attack. It stood with shabby pride in the middle of the block, a single light burning on the second floor of the building. Aside from that, its somber face was dark. Carella climbed to the top floor, trying to ignore the rustle of rats on the staircase, the hackles rising at the back of his neck. When he reached the fourth floor, he struck a match, found 4C at the far end of the hall and put his ear to the door, listening. To any casual passerby unfamiliar with the working ways of the police—and there were likely to be, oh, just *scores* of such passersby on a pitch-black landing at two o'clock in the morning—Carella might have looked like an eavesdropper, which is just what he was. He had been with the police department for a good many years, though, and he could not recall *ever* knocking on a door behind which there might be a criminal without first listening. He listened now for about five minutes, heard nothing, and only then knocked.

There was no answer.

He had decided together with Brown that his visit to Weinberg should not come as a visit from a cop. Instead, he was to pose as one of the "friends" Brown had hinted at, here to seek retribution for the beating Weinberg had possibly administered. The only problem seemed to be that no one was answering the door. Carella knocked again. Weinberg had earlier told Brown that he was about to curl up with a bottle of bourbon. Was it possible he had gone over to the Selby Arms, kicked Brown and the room around a little, and then returned here to his own little palace to knock off the bottle of cheer? Carella banged on the door a third time.

A door at the other end of the hall opened.

"Who is it there?" a woman's voice said.

"Friend of Al's," Carella answered.

"What you doing knocking down the door in the middle of the night?"

"Have to see him about something," Carella said. The landing was dark, and no light came from the woman's apartment. He strained to see her in the gloom, but could make out only a vague shape in the doorway, clothed in what was either a white nightgown or a white robe.

"He's probably asleep," the woman said, "same as everybody else around here."

"Yeah, why don't you just go do that yourself, lady?" Carella said.

"Punk," the woman replied, but she closed the door. Carella heard a lock being snapped, and then the heavy bar of a Fox lock being wedged against the door, solidly hooked into the steel plate that was screwed to the floor inside. He fished into his pocket, took out a penlight, flashed it onto Weinberg's lock, and then pulled out his ring of keys. He tried five keys before he found the one that opened the door. He slipped the key out of the lock, put the ring back into his pocket, gently eased the door open, went into the apartment, closed the door softly behind him, and stood breathing quietly in the darkness.

The room was as black as the landing had been.

A water tap dripped into a sink somewhere off on his left. On the street outside, a fire engine siren wailed into the night. He listened. He could see nothing, could hear nothing. Cupping his penlight in his hand, he flashed it only a few feet ahead of him and began moving into the room, vaguely making out a chair, a sofa, a television set. At the far end of the room, there was a closed door, presumably leading to the bedroom. He turned off the flash, stood silent and motionless for several moments while his eyes readjusted to the darkness, and then started for the bedroom door. He had moved not four feet when he tripped and fell forward, his hands coming out immediately to break his fall. His right hand sank to the wrist into something soft and gushy. He withdrew it immediately, his left hand thumbing the flash into light. He was looking into the wide-open eyes of Albert Weinberg. The something soft and gushy was a big bloody hole in Weinberg's chest.

Carella got to his feet, turned on the lights, and went into the small bathroom off the kitchen. When he turned on the lights there, an army of cockroaches scurried for cover. Fighting nausea, Carella washed his bloody right hand, dried it on a grimy towel hanging on a bar over the sink, and then went into the other room to call the precinct. A radio motor-patrol car arrived some five minutes later. Carella filled in the patrolmen, told them he'd be back shortly, and then headed crosstown and uptown to Irving Krutch's apartment. He did not get there until 3:15 A.M., two and a half hours before dawn.

Krutch opened the door the moment Carella gave his name. He was wearing pajamas, his hair was tousled, even his mustache looked as if it had been suddenly awakened from a very deep sleep.

"What's the matter?" he asked.

"Just a few questions, Mr. Krutch," Carella said.

"At three in the morning?"

"We're both awake, aren't we?"

"I wasn't two minutes ago," Krutch said. "Besides . . ."

"This won't take long," Carella said. "Did you speak to Arthur Brown tonight?"

"I did. Why? What . . .?"

"When was that?"

"Must have been about . . . eight o'clock? Eight-thirty? I really can't say for sure."

"What'd you talk about, Mr. Krutch?"

"Well Brown told me you'd found a piece of that photograph in Ehrbach's apartment, and he said you'd also got another piece from Weinberg. I was supposed to come up to the squadroom tomorrow morning and see them. In fact, *you* were supposed to show them to me."

"But you couldn't wait, huh?"

"What do you mean, I couldn't . . ,"

"Where'd you go after you spoke to Brown?"

"Out to dinner."

"Where?'

"The Ram's Head. The top of 777 Jefferson."

"Anybody with you?"

"Yes."

"Who?"

"A friend of mine."

"Man or woman?"

"A girl."

"What time'd you leave the restaurant?"

"About ten-thirty, I guess."

"Where'd you go?"

"For a walk. We looked in the store windows along Hall Avenue. It was a beautiful night and . . ."

"Where were you along about midnight, Mr. Krutch?"

"Here," Krutch said.

"Alone?"

"No."

"The girl came back here with you?"

"Yes."

"So she was with you between what time and what time?" Carella said.

"She was here when Brown called at eight—or whenever it was." Krutch paused. "She's still here."

"Where?"

"In bed."

"Get her up."

"Why?"

"One man's been assaulted and another's been killed," Carella said. "I want her to tell me where you were when all this was happening. That all right with you?"

"Who was killed?" Krutch asked.

"You sound as if you *know* who was *assaulted*," Carella said quickly.

"No. No, I don't."

"Then why'd you only ask who was killed? Aren't you interested in who was beaten up?"

"I'm . . ." Krutch paused. "Let me get her. She can clear this up in a minute."

"I hope so," Carella said.

Krutch went into the bedroom. Carella heard voices behind the closed door. The bedsprings creaked. There were footsteps. The door opened again. The girl was a young blonde, her long hair trailing down her back, her brown eyes wide and frightened. She was wearing a man's bathrobe belted tightly at the waist. Her hands fluttered like butterflies on an acid trip.

"This is Detective Carella," Krutch said. "He wants to know . . ."

"*I'll* ask her," Carella said. "What's your name, Miss?"

"Su . . . Su . . . Suzie," she said.

"Suzie what?"

"Suzie Endicott."

"What time did you get here tonight, Miss Endicott?"

"About . . . seven-thirty," she said. "Wasn't it seven-thirty, Irving?"

"About then," Krutch said.

"What time did you go out to dinner, Miss Endicott?"

"Eight or eight-thirty."

"Where'd you eat?"

"The Ram's Head."

"And where'd you go afterwards?"

"We walked for a little while, and then came here."

"What time was that?"

"I guess we got here at about eleven."

"Have you been here since?"

"Yes," she said.

"Did Mr. Krutch leave you at any time between seven-thirty and now?"

"Yes, when he went to the men's room at the restaurant," Suzie said.

"Happy now?" Krutch asked.

"Overjoyed," Carella answered. "Are you familiar with timetables, Mr. Krutch?"

"What do you mean? *Train* timetables?"

"No, *investigating* timetables. You're an insurance investigator, I though you might . . ."

"I'm not sure I'm following you."

"I want you to work up a timetable for me. I want you to list everything you did and the exact time you did it from 6 P.M. until right this minute," Carella said, and paused. "I'll wait," he added.

7

THERE'S nothing like a little homicide to give an investigation a shot in the arm. Or the chest, as the case may be. Albert Weinberg had been shot in the chest at close range with a .32-caliber pistol. His demise caused Brown to have a heated argument with the hospital intern who kept insisting he should be kept there under observation, and who refused to give him back his trousers. Brown called Carella, who brought his partner a pair of pants, a clean shirt, and his own spare gun. The two men had a hurried consultation while Brown dressed, deciding that Carella should go out to Calm's Point for a chat in Italian with Lucia Feroglio, the late Carmine Bonamico's sister-in-law. In the meantime, Brown would go over to the Ferguson Gallery, presumably closed on a Sunday, let himself into the place (against the law, but what the hell), and do a little snooping around. The nurse came in as Brown was zipping up his fly.

"What are you doing out of bed?" she asked.

"I'll get back in, if you'll join me," Brown said, grinning lecherously, and the nurse fled down the corridor, calling for the intern. By the time the intern got to the room, the detectives were in the main lobby downstairs, setting up plans for contacting each other later in the day. They nodded to each other briefly, and went out into the June sunshine to pursue their separate pleasures.

Carella's pleasure was the Church of the Holy Spirit on Inhurst Boulevard in Calm's Point. He had first stopped at Lucia Feroglio's garden apartment where he was told by her neighbors that the old lady went to nine o'clock Mass every Sunday morning. He had then driven over to the church, where Mass was in progress, and asked the sexton if he knew Lucia Feroglio, and if he would mind pointing her out when Mass broke. The sexton seemed not to understand any English until Carella put five dollars in the box in the narthex. The sexton then admitted that he knew Lucia Feroglio very well, and would be happy to identify her when she came out of the church.

Lucia must have been a beauty in her youth; Carella could not understand how or why she had remained a spinster. A woman in her seventies now, she still walked with a tall, erect pride, her hair snowy white, her features recalling those of ancient Roman royalty, the aquiline nose, the full sensuous mouth, the high brow and almond-shaped eyes. The sexton nodded toward her as she came down the broad sunwashed steps. Carella moved to her side immediately and said, *"Scusi, Signorina Feroglio?"*

The woman turned with a faint half-smile on her mouth, her eyebrows lifting in mild curiosity. *"Sì, che cosa?"* she asked.

"Mi chiamo Steve Carella," he answered. *"Sono un agente investigativo, dal distretto ottanta-sette."* He opened his wallet and showed her his detective's shield.

"Sì che vuole?" Lucia asked. "What do you want?"

"Possiamo parlare?" Carella asked. "Can we talk?"

"Certo," she said, and they began to walk away from the church together.

Lucia seemed to have no aversion to holding a conversation with a cop. She was warm, open, and cooperative, speaking in a Sicilian dialect Carella understood only incompletely, promising him she would tell him everything she knew about the photographic segment she had inherited from her sister. As it turned out, though, she knew nothing at *all* about it.

"I do not understand," Carella said in Italian. "Did you not tell the insurance investigator that the full picture reveals where the treasure is?"

"Ma che tesoro?" Lucia asked. "What treasure?"

"The treasure," Carella repeated. "Did you not tell Mr.

Krutch about a treasure? When you gave him the list and the photograph?"

"I know nothing of a treasure," Lucia said. "And *what* list? I gave him only the little piece of picture."

"You did *not* give him a list with names on it?"

"No. Nor has Mr. Krutch given me the thousand dollars he promised. Do you know this man?"

"Yes, I know him."

"Would you ask him, please, to send me my money? I gave him the picture, and now it is only fair to expect payment. I am not a wealthy woman."

"Let me understand this, Miss Feroglio," Carella said. "Are you telling me that you did *not* give Mr. Krutch a list of names?"

"Never. *Mai*. Never."

"And you did *not* tell Mr. Krutch about a treasure?"

"If I did not know it, how could I have told him?" She turned to him suddenly, and smiled warmly and quite seductively for a woman in her seventies. *Is* there a treasure, *signore?*" she asked.

"God only knows, *signorina*," Carella answered, and returned the smile.

The best burglars in the world are cops.

There are three types of alarm systems in general use, and the one on the back door of the Ferguson Gallery was a closed-circuit system, which meant that it could not be put out of commission merely by cutting the wires, as could be done with the cheapest kind. A weak current ran constantly through the wires of the closed-circuit system; if you cut them, breaking the current, the alarm would sound. So Brown cross-contacted the wires, and then opened the door with a celluloid strip. It was as simple as that, and it took him no longer than ten minutes. In broad daylight.

The gallery was empty and still.

Sunshine slanted silently through the wide plate-glass windows fronting Jefferson Avenue. The white walls were pristine and mute. The only screaming in the place came from the colorful paintings on the walls. Brown went immediately to the blue door on the far wall, opened it and stepped into Bramley Kahn's office.

He started with Kahn's desk. He found letters to and from artists, letters to patrons, a rough mock-up of a brochure announcing the gallery's one-man show to come in August, memos from Kahn to himself, a letter from a museum in Philadelphia, another from the Guggenheim in New York, a hardbound copy of *Story of O* (the first few pages of which Brown scanned, almost getting hooked, almost forgetting why he had come here), a trayful of red pencils and blue pencils, and in the bottom drawer a locked metal cashbox—and a .32-caliber Smith & Wesson. Brown tented his handkerchief over the revolver, picked it up by the butt, and sniffed the barrel. Despite the fact that Albert Weinberg, his late partner, had been slain with a .32-caliber weapon, this gun did not seem to have been fired lately. Brown rolled out the cylinder. There were six cartridges in the pistol, one in each chamber. He closed the gun, put it back into the drawer, and was reaching for the cashbox when the telephone rang. He almost leaped out of Steve Carella's borrowed trousers. The phone rang once, twice, again, again, again. It stopped suddenly.

Brown kept watching the instrument.

It began ringing again. It rang eight times. Then it stopped.

Brown waited.

The phone did not ring again.

He lifted the gray metal cashbox from the bottom drawer. The lock on it was a simple one; he opened the cashbox in thirty seconds. It contained anything but cash. He found a partnership agreement between Kahn and Geraldine Ferguson, a certificate for two hundred shares of IBM stock. Kahn's last will and testament, three United States Savings Bonds in fifty-dollar denominations, and a small, white, unmarked, unsealed envelope.

Brown opened the envelope. There was a slip of white paper in it:

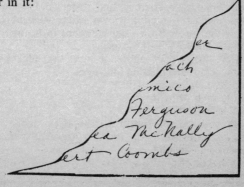

However lousy a bank robber Carmine Bonamico may have been, he was sure good at cutting out paper dolls. If this wasn't the second half of the list Krutch had brought to the squadroom, Brown would eat the list, the photograph, the first chapter of *Story of O,* and maybe O herself. He quickly copied the names in his notebook, replaced the fragment in its envelope, put the envelope and everything else back into the cashbox, locked the box, and replaced it in the bottom drawer of the desk. His attention was captured by the painting of the nude on the opposite wall. He went to it, lifted one edge, and peeked behind it. Reaching up with both hands, he took the heavy painting off the wall. There was a small black safe behind it. Brown knew that people who used safes or combination locks with any frequency would often leave the dial just a notch or two to the right or left of the last number. This facilitated constant opening, since all you then had to do was give the dial a single twist each time, rather than going through the whole, boring rigmarole. He was moving the dial a notch to the left of the number showing when he heard the back door of the gallery being opened. Swiftly, he moved behind the door of Kahn's office, and threw back his jacket.

The butt of Carella's borrowed .38 protruded from a holster at his waist. He drew the gun now and stood silently listening to the footsteps that clattered across the white tile floor toward Kahn's office. The footsteps stopped just outside the open door. Brown held his breath. The man was in the doorway now, his shadow falling into the room across the gray rug. Brown did not want the man to be Bramley Kahn. Breaking and entry was breaking and entry, and Brown did not want a suit filed against the city; Brown did not want to get kicked off the force; Brown did not want to be smothered again by the ghetto he had escaped.

The first things that registered were the thick handlebar mustache and the glinting blue eyes.

"Hello Krutch," Brown said.

Irving Krutch whirled.

"Hey," he said. "Hi."

"Didn't you see that decal on the back door? 'These premises are protected by the Buckley Alarm System.'"

"I cross-contacted the wiring," Krutch said.

"That makes two of us. Was it you who called ten minutes ago?"

"Yes. I wanted to make sure nobody was here."

"Somebody *was* here," Brown said.

"So I see."

"What do you want, Krutch?"

"The same thing you want. We're in this together, re-member?"

"I thought you were letting *us* handle it."

"I figured you might need a hand."

Brown holstered the gun, went to the safe again, moved the dial a notch to the left, then two notches, then three, trying to open it after each move, and getting no results. He tried the same sequence to the right, and when he got nothing, he turned to Krutch and said, "I *do* need a hand. Grab one end of this painting."

"Have you found anything?" Krutch asked.

Brown hesitated. "No," he said.

They lifted the painting and hung it in place. Brown stepped back from it, walked over to the wall again, and tilted one corner of the frame.

"A little to the other side," Krutch said.

"How's that?"

"Perfect."

"Let's go," Brown said.

"I'd sure like to know what's in that safe," Krutch said.

"So would I. What's your guess?"

"A little piece of a picture."

"How are you on safecracking?"

"Lousy."

"So am I. Let's go."

"Where are we going?" Krutch asked.

"*You're* going to fix those alarm wires. *I'm* going to visit Geraldine Ferguson."

"Fix the wires? I can get arrested if I'm caught do-ing that."

"I may arrest you, anyway," Brown said. "You're in here illegally."

"So are you."

"An off-duty cop on the prowl. Cruising by, saw the back door ajar, came in and discovered a burglary in progress."

"I'm your *partner,*" Krutch protested.

"I had another partner, too. Albert Weinberg, who right now is on ice downtown."

"I had nothing to do with that," Krutch said.

"Who suggested you did?"

"Carella."

"Well, maybe he's just a suspicious person," Brown said.

"How about *you?* What do *you* think?"

"I think you were with a young lady named Suzie Endicott from seven-thirty until whenever it was Carella came to see you. That's what you told him, isn't it?"

"Yes."

"So why would I have any reason to doubt you?"

"Look, Brown . . ."

"I'm looking."

"I want that lost N.S.L.A. money; I want it very badly. But not badly enough to kill for it. *Nothing's* worth that much. Not even my career."

"Okay."

"I just want to get that straight between us."

"It's straight," Brown said. "Now let's get the hell out of here."

Geraldine Ferguson was in her pajamas when she opened the door.

"Oh, hell," she said.

"That's right, Miss Ferguson," Brown said. "Here come de fuzz."

"He's *admitting* it," she said in surprise, and then smiled. "Come in. I admire honest men."

The living room resembled an annex to the gallery—white walls, muted furniture, huge canvases glaring with color, twisted sculptured shapes on pedestals. Gerry swayed across the rug like a dancer, tight little behind jiggling in the blue silk pajama bottoms, black hair caught in a pony tail that bounced between her shoulder blades.

"Would you like a drink?" she asked. "Or is it too early?"

"It's almost one o'clock," Brown said.

"Name it."

"I'm on duty."

"So? When did cops get so lily-white, you should pardon the expression?"

"I like to keep a clear head when I'm working," Brown said.

"Okay, keep a clear head," Gerry said, and shrugged. *"I'll* have a drink, though, if you don't mind. I find Sundays very boring. Once I've read the comics and Martin Levin, there's just nothing exciting left to do."

"Who's Martin Levin?" Brown asked.

Gerry went to a bar over which hung a white canvas

slashed with jagged black streaks of paint. She poured a liberal shot of bourbon onto the ice in a short glass, lifted the glass, said, "Here's to improved race relations," and drank, eying him steadily over the glass.

"Miss Ferguson . . ."

"Gerry," she corrected.

"Gerry, a man was killed last night . . ."

"Who?" she said immediately, and put the glass down on the bartop.

"The man who visited you several times. The one who said he was Al Reynolds. Or Al Randolph."

"What was his real name?"

"Albert Weinberg." Brown paused. "Ever hear of him?"

"No," Gerry said, and picked up her glass again. "What's *your* real name?"

"Arthur Brown."

"You're putting me on," she said, and smiled.

"No, that's it. Detective Second/Grade, 87th Squad. Want to see my shield?"

"Why?"

"You're supposed to ask for identification."

"I don't like to do anything I'm *supposed* to do," Gerry said.

"On Wednesday night . . ."

"How'd we get back to Wednesday?"

"I just took us there," Brown said impatiently. "On Wednesday night, two men killed each other in a brawl . . ."

"Who?"

"That's not important, Gerry. What *is* important is that one of them had a piece of a photograph in his hand . . ."

"Are we going to start on *that* again? I already told you . . ."

"Miss Ferguson," Brown said, "I've got some questions to ask you concerning murder and armed robbery. I'd like to ask those questions here in comfortable surroundings, but I can just as easily ask them uptown, in the squadroom."

"What's that, a threat?"

"No, it's a realistic appraisal of the situation."

"After I was nice enough to offer you a drink," Gerry said, and smiled. "Go on, I promise to be quiet."

"Thank you. We have good reason to believe that the fragment in the dead man's hand was part of a larger

photograph showing the location of the money stolen
from the National Savings & Loan Association six years
ago. We also have good reason to believe that *you* have
another piece of that picture, and *we* want it. It's as simple as that."

"What smoked you out, Arthur?" she asked. "What
made you drop the phony cover? Are you afraid somebody else might get killed?"

"It's possible, yes."

"Me?"

"Possibly. *Whoever's* got a piece of that picture is in
danger. For your own safety . . ."

"Bullshit," Gerry said.

"I beg your pardon?"

"The day the cops start worrying about anybody's
safety is the day . . ." She banged the glass down on
the bar top. "Who do you think you're kidding, Arthur?"

"Miss Ferguson, I'm not . . ."

"And make up your goddamn mind! It's either Miss
Ferguson or it's Gerry. You can't have it both ways."

"Then I think I'd prefer Miss Ferguson."

"Why? Are you afraid of me or something? Big strong
Superspade afraid of a snippety little girl?"

"Let's knock off the 'Superspade' crap, shall we?"
Brown said.

"You ever been to bed with a white girl?" Gerry asked
suddenly.

"No."

"Want to try?"

"No."

"Why not?"

"Believe it or not, Miss Ferguson, my fantasies don't
include a big black Cadillac and a small white blonde."

"I'm not a blonde."

"I know that. I was merely . . ."

"Stop getting so nervous. I'll bet your palms are wet."

"My palms are dry," Brown said evenly.

"Mine aren't," Gerry said, and turned away from him
to pour herself another drink. The living room was silent.
"You married?" she asked.

"I am."

"That's okay. I've been to bed with married spades,
too."

"I don't like that expression, Miss Ferguson."

"Which? Married?" she asked, and turned to face him,
leaning on the bar. "Grow up, Arthur."

Brown rose from the sofa. "I think maybe we'd *better* head uptown," he said. "You want to get dressed, please?"

"No, I don't," Gerry said, and smiled, and sipped at her bourbon. "What'll the charge be? Attempted rape?"

"I don't have to charge you with anything, Miss Ferguson. I'm conducting a murder investigation, and I'm entitled . . ."

"All right, all right, don't start spouting legalities. Sit down, Arthur. Oh, *do* sit down. I'd much rather talk here than in some stuffy old squadroom."

Brown sat.

"There, isn't that better? Now—what would you like to know?"

"Do you have a piece of the photograph?"

"Yes."

"Where'd you get it?"

"My brother-in-law gave it to me."

"Louis D'Amore?"

"Yes."

"When?"

"Just before the holdup."

"What'd he say about it?"

"Only that I should hold onto it."

"How come he gave it to you, and not your sister?"

"My sister's a scatterbrain, always was. Lou knew who the smart one was."

"Did he give you the list, too?"

"What list?"

"The list of names."

"I don't know anything about a list of names."

"That's a lie, Gerry."

"No, I swear. What list?"

"A list that has your name on it, among others."

"I've never seen it."

"You're lying Gerry. Your partner has half of that list. Where'd he get it?"

"I don't know anything *about* a list. What's it supposed to be?"

"Forget it," Brown said. "Where's your part of the snapshot?"

"In the gallery safe."

"Will you turn it over to us?"

"No."

"I thought you said . . ."

"I said I'd answer your questions. Okay. I've done

that. There's no law that says I have to give personal property to the police."

"I can think of one," Brown said.

"Yeah, which one?"

"How about Section 1308 of the Penal Law? *A person who conceals, withholds, or aids in concealing or withholding any property, knowing the same to have been stolen . . .*"

"Is the photograph stolen property?"

"It indicates the *location* of stolen property."

"How do I know that? Lou gave me a tiny little corner of a photograph and asked me to hold onto it. That's all I know."

"Okay, I'm *telling* you the photograph shows the location of the N.S.L.A. loot. Now you know."

"Can you prove it?" Gerry said, and smiled. "I don't think so, Arthur. Until you find the money, you can't say for sure it even *exists*. And you *won't* find the money until you put the whole picture together. Tch, tch, such a dilemma. Why don't we go into the other room and ball a little?"

"I'd rather not, thanks."

"I'd drive you out of your mind, Arthur."

"You already have," Brown said, and left.

8

THE DILEMMA was not quite so horned as Geraldine
Ferguson imagined. All Brown had to do was find himself a Supreme Court judge, swear to the judge that upon
reliable information and personal knowledge, there was
probable cause to believe that a safe at the Ferguson
Gallery at 568 Jefferson Avenue contained evidence that
could lead to the solution of a crime, and request from
the judge a warrant and order of seizure to open the safe,
search it, and appropriate the evidence. He couldn't do
that today because it was Sunday, and in the city for
which Brown worked, Supreme Court judges were entitled to a day of rest; only the direst of emergencies
would have been considered cause for shaking a man
out of his bed and requesting a search warrant. Brown
was confident, though, that Gerry would not rush down
to the gallery and take the photograph out of the safe.
He had done nothing to disabuse her notion that he
was helpless to open that safe, and he felt certain the
photograph would still be there come morning when,
armed with his legal paper, he would force her to pro-
duce it.

At 3 P.M. Sunday afternoon, he met with Carella in the
squadroom and went over what they now had. By com-
bining Krutch's half of the list (which *he* claimed to
have received from Lucia Feroglio, but which *she*
claimed she had not given him) with the half found in
Kahn's cashbox (which Geraldine Ferguson claimed she
knew nothing about), they were able to piece together
seven names:

> ALBERT WEINBERG
>
> DONALD RENNINGER
>
> EUGENE E. EHRBACH
>
> ALICE BONAMICO

GERALDINE FERGUSON

DOROTHEA MCNALLY

ROBERT COOMBS

The first four people on the list were already dead. The fifth person had admitted having a piece of the photograph, and they hoped to get that from her in the morning. Now, with the telephone directories for the five sections of the city spread open before them, they began searching for the remaining two names.

There was a Robert Coombs in Riverhead, and another Robert Coombs in Bethtown.

There were a hundred and sixty-four McNallys scattered all over the city, more than enough to have started a revival of the clan, but none of them were named Dorothea, and there was only one listing for a *McNally, D.*—on South Homestead, off Skid Row.

"How do you want to hit them?" Carella asked.

"Let's save Bethtown till tomorrow morning. Have to take a ferry to get out there, and God knows how they run on Sundays."

"Okay," Carella said. "Why don't I take the Coombs in Riverhead, and go straight home from there?"

"Fine. I'll take the McNally woman."

"How come you're getting all the girls lately?"

"It's only fair," Brown said. "We *never* get them on television."

It was a city of contrasts.

Follow Esplanade Avenue uptown to where the Central & Northeastern railroad tracks came up out of the ground and, within the length of a city block, the neighborhood crumbled before your eyes, buildings with awnings and doormen giving way to grimy brick tenements, well-dressed affluent citizens miraculously transformed into shabby, hungry, unemployed victims of poverty. Take any crosstown street that knifed through the 87th Precinct, follow it across Mason, and Culver, and Ainsley, and you passed through slums that spread like cancers and then abruptly shriveled on the fringes of fancy Silvermine Road, with luxurious, exclusive, wooded, moneyed Smoke Rise only a stone's throw away. Head all the way downtown to The Quarter, and find yourself a bustling middle-class bohemian community with its fair share of faggots and artsy-craftsy leather shops, its little theaters and renovated brownstones glistening with sandblasted facades and freshly painted balustrades and fire escapes, shuttered windows, cobblestoned alleys, spring flowers hanging in gaily colored pots over arched doorways with shining brass knobs and knockers. Then follow your nose west into Little Italy, a ghetto as dense as those uptown, but of a different hue, take a sniff of coffee being brewed in *espresso* machines, savor the rich smells of a transplanted Neapolitan cuisine merged with the aroma of roasting pork wafting over from Chinatown, not a block away, where the telephone booths resembled miniature pagodas and where the phones— like their uptown cousins—rarely worked. (How nice to have an emergency number with which to dial the police, three fast digits and a cop was on your doorstep— if only the phones would work.) Then walk a few blocks south, crossing the wide avenue where the elevated train structure used to stand, its shadow gone now, the flophouses and soup kitchens, the wholesale lighting fixture, restaurant supply, factory reject, party favor, and office equipment establishments draped with winos and exposed in all their shabby splendor to the June sunshine.

D. McNally lived in a building two blocks south of the wide avenue that ran for better than half a mile, the city's skid row, a graveyard for vagrants and drunks, a happy hunting ground for policemen anxious to fill arrest quotas—pull in a bum, charge him with vagrancy or disorderly conduct, allow him to spend a night or two or more in jail, and then turn him out into the street again, a much better person for his experience. Brown walked past two drunks who sat morosely on the front stoop. Neither of the men looked up at him. Sitting on the curb in front of the building, his feet in the gutter, was a third man. He had taken off his shirt, black with lice, and he delicately picked the parasites from the cloth now, squashing them with his thumbnail against the curbstone. His skin was a pale sickly white in the glare of the sunshine, his back and arms covered with sores.

The entryway was dark; after the brilliant sunshine outside, it hit the eyes like a closed fist. Brown studied the row of broken mailboxes and found one with a hand-crayoned card that read D. McNally, Apt. 2A. He climbed the steps, listened outside the apartment door for several moments, and then knocked.

"Yes?" a woman's voice said.

"Miss McNally?"

"Yes?" she said, and before Brown could announce that he was The Law, the door opened. The woman

standing in the doorway was perhaps fifty years old. Her
hair had been dyed a bright orange, and it exploded
about her chalk-white face like Fourth-of-July fireworks,
erupting from her scalp in every conceivable direction,
wildly unkempt, stubbornly independent. Her eyes were a
faded blue, their size emphasized by thick black liner.
Her lashes had been liberally stroked with mascara, her
brows had been darkened with pencil, her mouth had
been enlarged with lipstick the color of human blood.
She wore a silk flowered wrapper belted loosely at the
waist. Pendulous white breasts showed in the open top
of the wrapper. Near the nipple of one breast, a human
bite mark was clearly visible, purple against her very
white skin. She was a short, dumpy woman with an
overabundance of flabby flesh, and she looked as though
she had deliberately dressed for the role of the unre-
generate old whore in the local amateur production of
Seven Hookers East.

"I don't take niggers," she said immediately, and
started to close the door. Brown stuck his foot out, and
the closing door collided with his shoe. Through the narrow open crack, D. McNally said again, emphatically this
time, "I told you I don't take niggers." Brown didn't
know whether to laugh himself silly or fly into an offended rage. Here was a run-down old prostitute who
would probably flop with anyone and everyone for the
price of a bottle of cheap wine, but she would not take
Negroes. He decided to find it amusing.

"All I want's a blow job," he said.

"No," D. McNally said, alarmed now. "No. Go away!"

"A friend of mine sent me," he said.

From behind the door, D. McNally's voice lowered in
suspicion. "Which friend?" she asked. "I don't suck no
niggers."

"Lieutenant Byrnes," Brown said.

"A soldier?"

"No, a policeman," Brown said, and decided to end
the game. "I'm a detective, lady, you want to open this
door?"

"You ain't no detective," she said.

Wearily, Brown dug into his pocket and held his shield
up to the crack between door and jamb.

"Why didn't you say so?" D. McNally asked.

"Why? Do you suck nigger *detectives?*"

"I didn't mean no offense," she said, and opened the
door. "Come in."

He went into the apartment. It consisted of a tiny kitchen and a room with a bed. Dishes were piled in the sink, the bed was unmade, there was the stale stink of human sweat and cheap booze and cheaper perfume.

"You the Vice Squad?" she asked.

"No."

"I ain't hooking no more," she said. "That's why I told you to go away. I been out of the game, oh, must be six, seven months now."

"Sure," Brown said. "Is your name Dorothea McNally?"

"That's right. I put 'D. McNally' in the phone book and in the mailbox downstairs because there's all kinds of crazy nuts in this city, you know? Guys who call up and talk dirty, you know? I don't like that kind of dirty shit."

"No, I'll bet you don't."

"When I was hooking, I had a nice clientele."

"Mm-huh."

"Gentlemen."

"But no niggers."

"Look, you didn't take offense at that, did you?"

"No, of course not. Why should I take offense at a harmless little remark like that?"

"If you're going to make trouble just because I said . . ."

"I'm not going to make any trouble, lady."

"Because if you *are*, look, I'll go down on you right this minute, you know what I mean? A cock's a cock," Dorothea said, "white *or* black."

"Or even purple," Brown said.

"Sure, even purple. Just don't make trouble for me, that's all." She paused. "You want me to?"

"No. Thanks a lot," Brown said.

"Well," she said, and shrugged, "if you should change your mind . . ."

"I'll let you know. Meanwhile, I'm here to talk about a photograph."

"Yeah, well come on in," she said, gesturing toward the bedroom. "No sense standing here with the dirty dishes, huh?"

They walked into the other room. Dorothea sat on the bed and crossed her legs. Brown stood at the foot of the bed, looking down at her. She had allowed the silk wrapper to fall open again. The bite mark near her nipple looked angry and swollen, the outline of the teeth stitched across her flabby breast in a small elongated oval.

"A photograph, huh?" Dorothea said.

"That's right."

"Man, you guys sure know how to bring up ancient history," she said. "I thought you weren't going to make trouble for me."

"I'm not."

"I musta posed for those pictures twenty years ago. You mean to tell me one of them's still around?" She shook her head in amazement. "I was *some* little piece in those days. I had guys coming to see me all the way from San Francisco. They'd get in town, pick up the phone, 'Hello there, Dorothea, this is old Bruce, you ready to go, honey?' I was always ready to go in those days. I knew how to show a man a good time." she looked up at Brown. "I *still* do, I mean I'm not exactly what you'd call an old hag, you know. Not that I'm in the game, any more. I mean, I'm just saying."

"When was your last arrest for prostitution?" Brown asked.

"I told you, musta been six or seven . . ."

"Come on, I can check it."

"All right, last month. But I've been clean since. This is no kind of life for a person like me. So, you know, when you come around bringing up those pictures, Jesus, I can get in real trouble for something like that, can't I?" She smiled suddenly. "Why don't you just come on over here, sweetie, and we'll forget all about those pictures, okay?"

"The picture I'm talking about isn't pornography," Brown said.

"No? What then?"

"A picture that may have come into your possession six years ago."

"Jesus, who can remember six years ago?"

"You just now had no trouble remembering *twenty* years ago."

"Yeah, but that was . . . you know, a girl remembers something like that. That's the only time I ever done anything like that, you know, pose for pictures with some guy. I only let them take one roll, that was all, just *one,* and I got fifty bucks for it, which was more than I'd have got if I was just turning a trick without them taking pictures, you understand?"

"Sure," Brown said. "What do you know about the

National Savings & Loan Association holdup six years ago?"

"Oh, man, now we're jumping around real fast," Dorothea said. "First it's hooking, then it's dirty pictures, now it's armed robbery. The stakes keep getting higher all the time."

"What do you know about that holdup?"

"I think I remember reading about it."

"What do you remember reading?"

"Look . . . I got your word you ain't going to make trouble?"

"You've got it."

"My nephew was one of the guys who pulled that job."

"What's his name?"

"Peter Ryan. He's dead now. They *all* got killed on that job, some bank robbers," she said, and grimaced.

"And the picture?"

"What picture? I don't know what . . ."

"A piece of a snapshot. From what you've just told me, your nephew might have given it to you. Before the job. Would you remember anything like that?"

"Jesus, that was six years ago."

"Try to remember."

"When was the job? Do you remember what month it was?"

"August."

"August. Six years ago. Let me see . . ." She grimaced again. "I wasn't even living here at the time. God knows *where* the hell I was."

"Think, Dorothea."

"I think better when I'm drinking," she said.

"Have you got anything in the house?"

"Yeah, but that's like my insurance, you know? The Johns are few and far between these days."

Brown reached into his wallet. "Here's ten dollars," he said. "Drink up your insurance and get yourself another bottle later."

"And if I remember about the picture?"

"What about it?"

"How much is it worth to you?"

"Another twenty."

"Make it fifty. You're taking up a lot of my time, you know."

"I don't see a line of guys outside the door," Brown said.

"Well, they come and go, come and go," Dorothea

said. "I'd hate to have to send a trick away just because
I'm busy in here with a cop." She paused, and then
smiled. "Fifty?"

"Thirty-five."

"It's a deal." She went into the kitchen, took a bottle
of cheap rye from the shelf, poured herself a half tumbler-
ful, looked up, and said, "You want some of this piss?
Makes you go blind, I understand."

"No, thanks," Brown said.

"Here's looking up your whole family," Dorothea said,
and drained the glass. "Whooo," she said, "that's poison,
absolute poison." She poured the glass full to the brim
and carried it back into the bedroom with her. "I don't
remember any snapshot," she said, shaking her head.

"Where were you living at the time?"

"Up on the North Side, I think. I think I had a room
in a hotel up there." She sipped at the rye thoughtfully.
"Six years ago. That's like a whole century, you know?"

"Think."

"I'm thinking, just shut up. My nephew was in and
out all the time; who remembers whether he ever gave
me a snapshot?"

"This would be just a *portion* of a snapshot. Not the
whole picture."

"Better yet," Dorothea said. "Even if he *did* give it to
me, you know how many times I moved in the past
six years? Don't ask. Between The Law and the rent
collector, I'm a very busy lady."

"Where do you keep your valuables?"

"*What* valuables?"

"Where do you keep important papers?"

"Are you kidding me?"

"Things like your birth certificate, your Social Security
card . . ."

"Oh, yeah, I got them around someplace," Dorothea
said, and sipped at the drink again.

"Where?"

"I don't keep much junk, you know. I don't like
memories. Too many fucking memories," she said, and
this time she took a healthy swallow of the drink, drain-
ing the glass. She got up from the bed, walked into the
kitchen, and poured the glass full again. "You ever hear
of a fighter named Tiger Willis?" she asked, coming back
into the bedroom.

"No."

"This was before your time, I guess. Twenty-five years

ago, maybe even longer. He was a middleweight."

"What about him?"

"I used to live with him. He had a *shlong* on him, man,
it musta been a yard long." Dorothea shook her head.
"He got killed in the ring. This kid from Buenos Aires
killed him. Hit him so hard, he . . . I was there that
night, at ringside, you know. Freddie—that was his real
name, Freddie Willis, the 'Tiger' shit was just for the
ring—Freddie always got me a ringside seat for his
fights, I was something in those days, I was real mer-
chandise. This kid from Buenos Aires, he brought one up
from the floor, almost knocked Freddie's head off. And
Freddie went down, he went down like a stone, he hit that
canvas so hard . . ." She swallowed more rye and looked
away from Brown. "Well, those are the old times," she
said.

"About the photograph," Brown said gently.

"Yeah, yeah, the fucking photograph. Let me see
what's in the closet here."

She went across the room, and opened the door to the
closet. A black cloth coat hung on a wire hanger. Beside
it was a blue satin dress. Nothing else was hanging on
the wooden bar. On the floor of the closet, there were
two pairs of high-heeled pumps. A cardboard box and a
candy tin were on the shelf over the bar. Dorothea
reached up, and came back to the bed with the candy tin
in her hands. She pried off the lid.

"Not much here," she said. "I don't like to keep things."

There was a birth certificate, a marriage certificate
(Dorothea Pierce to Richard McNally), a snip of hair in
a cheap gold-plated locket, a *Playbill* for an opening
night long long ago, a photograph of a very young girl
sitting on a swing behind a clapboard house, a faded
valentine card, and a copy of *Ring* magazine with a picture of Tiger Willis on the cover.

"That's all of it," Dorothea said.

"Want to dump it all on the bed here?" Brown suggested. "What we're looking for may be very small." He
picked up the *Playbill* and shook out its pages. Nothing.
He picked up the copy of *Ring* magazine.

"Be careful with that," Dorothea warned.

He gave it a single shake. The pages fluttered apart,
and a glossy black-and-white photograph scrap fell onto
the soiled sheets.

"Is that what you're looking for?' Dorothea asked.

"That's what I'm looking for," Brown said.

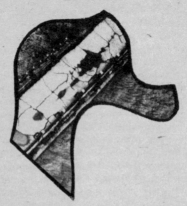

"It resembles Donald Duck," she said. "Or Woody Woodpecker."

"Or the extinct dodo bird," Brown said.

"I don't remember Petey giving it to me," Dorothea said, and shook her head. "I suppose he must have, but I really don't remember." Her look hardened. She held out her hand to Brown, and said, "That's thirty-five bucks, mister."

The address for the Robert Coombs who lived in Riverhead was 6451 Avondale, two miles from Carella's house. Carella got there at about four-thirty, pulling into the tree-lined street just behind a Good Humor ice-cream truck, the first he had seen this season. The houses on the block were mostly two-family homes. The community gave an appearance of neat lower-middle-class respectability. This was Sunday afternoon, and the Riverhead burghers were out on their front stoops reading their newspapers or listening to transistor radios. Carella counted twelve kids on bicycles as he drove up the street searching for 6451.

The house was on the corner of Avondale and Birch, a big brick-and-clapboard building on a comfortable plot. As Carella stepped out of the car, he smelled the aroma of cooking steak. He had eaten only a hamburger for lunch, and he was hungry as hell. A small black sign on the front lawn was lettered in white with the name R. COOMBS. Carella went up the walk to the front door, rang the bell, and waited. There was no answer. He rang again. He waited several moments more, and then walked around toward the back of the house. A man in

a white apron was standing near an outdoor grille, a long
fork in his right hand. Another man and two women were
sitting at a redwood picnic table opposite the grille. The
foursome was in conversation as Carella came around the
side of the house, but they stopped talking the moment
they saw him.

"I'm looking for Robert Coombs," Carella said.

"Yes, I'm Coombs," the man at the grille said.

"Sorry to intrude like this, Mr. Coombs," Carella said,
walking over to him. "I'm Detective Carella of the 87th
Squad. I wonder if I might talk to you privately."

"What is it, Bobby?" one of the women said, and rose
immediately from where she was sitting at the picnic
table. She was a tall woman wearing a blond fall, a snug
blue cashmere sweater, tight navy-blue slacks. Her eyes
were a shade lighter than the sweater, and she squinted
them in suspicion, if not open hostility, as she approached
the grille. "I'm *Mrs.* Coombs," she said, as if she were
announcing exactly who ran this household. "What is it
you want?"

"He's a detective, hon," Coombs said.

"A detective? What is it? What's the matter?"

"Nothing, Mrs. Coombs," Carella said. "I simply
wanted to ask your husband some questions."

"What about? Are you in some kind of trouble, Bobby?"

"No, no, hon, I . . ."

"He's not in any trouble, Mrs. Coombs. This has to do
with . . ."

"Then it can wait," Mrs. Coombs said. "The steaks are
almost done. You just come back later, Detective . . ."

"Coppola," Coombs said.

"Carella," Carella said.

"We're about to eat," Mrs. Coombs said. "You come
back later, do you hear?"

"Can you come back in an hour?" Coombs asked
gently.

"Make it an hour and a half," Mrs. Coombs snapped.

"Honey, an hour's more time than . . ."

"I don't want to rush through my Sunday dinner," Mrs.
Coombs said flatly. "An hour and a half, Detective Coppola."

"Carella," he said, *"bon appètitè,"* and walked out of
the yard, the aroma of the cooking steak nearly destroy-
ing him forever. He found an open luncheonette on Birch,
ordered a cup of coffee and a cheese Danish, and then
went out for a stroll around the neighborhood. Four

little girls on the sidewalk ahead were skipping rope, chanting their ritualistic ditty, "Double-ee-Dutch, double-ee-Dutch," and from the open lot on the corner, there came the crack of a bat against a baseball, and a shout went up from the middle-aged men in shirt sleeves who were watching their sons play. The sky, magnificently blue all day long, virtually cloudless, was succumbing to the pale violet of dusk. The balmy afternoon breeze was turning a bit cooler. All up and down the street, he could hear mothers calling their children in to dinner. It was the time of day when a man wanted to be home with his family. Carella looked at his watch and sighed.

Isabel Coombs was a ventriloquist, of that Carella was certain.

The Coombs's guests had gone indoors the moment he'd returned, and he could see them now through the rear sliding glass doors of the house, standing near the record player and browsing through the album collection. He sat with Mr. and Mrs. Coombs at the redwood table and even though Robert Coombs occasionally tried to answer a question, he was really only the dummy in the act, and Isabel Coombs was doing most of the talking.

"Mr. Coombs," Carella said, "I'll make this as brief as I can. We found your name on a list allegedly . . ."

"His name?" Isabel said. "You found *Bobby's* name on some list?"

"Yes, ma'am," Carella said, "a list . . ."

"*His* name is not on any list," Isabel said.

"Well, maybe it is, hon," Robert said.

"It is *not*," Isabel said. "Detective Caretta . . ."

"Carella."

"Yes, perhaps before we talk any further, we'd better get a lawyer."

"Well, that's entirely up to you, of course," Carella said, "but there's no intention here of charging your husband with any crime. We're merely seeking information about . . ."

"Then why is his name on a *list?*" Isabel demanded.

Carella's wife was a deaf mute. He looked at Isabel Coombs now, wearing her blond fall and her brassy voice, and silently contrasted her with Teddy—black hair and brown eyes, voiceless, gentle, beautiful.

Mrs. Coombs's blue eyes flashed. "Well?" she said.

"Mrs. Coombs," Carella said patiently, "maybe it'd be better if you just let me *ask* the questions before you decide what they're going to be."

"What's that supposed to mean?"

"It's supposed to mean that this can take ten minutes or ten hours. We can do it right here in your back yard, or I can request that your husband accompany me . . ."

"You're going to *arrest* him?"

"No, ma'am, I'm only going to ask him some questions."

"Then why don't you?"

Carella was silent for a moment. Then he said only, "Yes, ma'am," and fell silent again. He had forgotten for a moment just what it was he wanted to ask Coombs. He kept thinking of Teddy and wishing he were home in bed with her. "Well," he said, "Mr. Coombs, would you have any knowledge of a robbery that took place . . .?"

"I thought you said there wasn't any crime being investigated," Isabel said.

"I didn't say that. I said we had no intention of charging your *husband* with any crime."

"You just now mentioned a robbery."

"Yes, six years ago." He turned to Robert and said, "Would you know anything about such a robbery, Mr. Coombs?"

"I don't know," Robert said. "Who was robbed?"

"The National Savings & Loan Association."

"What's that?"

"A bank."

"Where?"

"In this city," Carella said. "Downtown."

"Six years ago," Isabel said flatly, "we were living in Detroit."

"I see," Carella said. "And when did you move here?"

"Just before Christmas," Robert said.

"That'd be . . . about six months ago."

"Almost six months ago exactly," Robert said.

"Mr. Coombs, did anyone ever give you or did you ever come into possession in any way whatsoever . . ."

"This has to do with the robbery, doesn't it?" Isabel said shrewdly.

". . . a piece of a photograph?" Carella continued, ignoring her.

"What do you mean?" Robert asked.

"A section of a picture."

"A picture of *what?*" Isabel asked.

"We don't know. That is, we're not sure."

"Then how would my husband know whether or not he

has it?"

"If he has it, I guess he would know he has it," Carella said. "Do you have it?"

"No," Robert said.

"Do any of these names mean anything to you? Carmine Bonamico, Louis D'Amore . . ."

"No."

"Jerry Stein . . ."

"No."

"Pete Ryan?"

"No."

"Never heard of any of them?"

"No. Who are they?"

"How about these names? Albert Weinberg, Donald Renninger, Alice Bonamico . . ."

"No, none of them."

"Dorothea McNally? Geraldine Ferguson?"

Robert shook his head.

"Eugene Ehrbach?"

"No, I'm sorry."

"Well, then," Carella said. "I guess that's it. Thank you very much for your time." He rose, nodded briefly at Isabel Coombs, and started out of the yard.

Behind him, Isabel said, "Is that all?"

She sounded disappointed.

Carella did not get home until eight o'clock that night. His wife Teddy was sitting at the kitchen table with Arthur Brown. She smiled as he entered, brown eyes engulfing him, one delicate hand brushing a strand of black hair away from her face.

"Hey, this is a surprise," he said to Brown. "Hello, honey," he said to Teddy, and bent to kiss her.

"How'd you make out?" Brown asked.

"He's not our man. Moved here from Detroit six months ago, doesn't know a thing about the photograph, and never even *heard* of National Savings & Loan." Carella suddenly turned to his wife. "I'm sorry honey," he said, "I didn't realize my back was turned." He repeated what he had just told Brown, watching Teddy's eyes for confirmation that she was reading his lips. She nodded when he finished, and then rapidly moved her fingers in the hand alphabet he understood, telling him that Arthur had found another section of the photograph.

"Is that right?" Carella said, turning to Brown. "You've got another piece?"

"That's why I'm here, baby," Brown said. He reached into his jacket pocket, pulled out a glassine envelope, opened it, and emptied five pieces of the snapshot onto the tabletop. The men stared blankly at the collection. Teddy Carella—who lived in a soundless, speechless, largely visual and tactile universe—studied the twisted shapes on the tabletop. Her hands moved out swiftly. In less time than it had taken Carella to assemble the four pieces that had been in their possession yesterday, she now put together the five pieces before her:

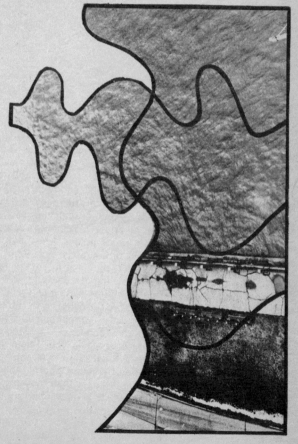

"Hey!" Brown said. *"Now* we're getting there!"
"Yeah," Carella said, "but where?"

9

NEVER let it be bruited about that just because a homicide victim also happens to be an ex-con, the police will devote less time and energy to finding out who has done him in. Perish the thought! In this fair and democratic land of ours, the rich and the poor, the powerful and the meek, the honest citizen and the wrongdoer are all afforded equal protection under the law, even after they're dead. So, boy oh boy, did those guys work hard trying to find out who had left the hole in Albert Weinberg's chest!

To begin with, there are a lot of people who have to be informed when someone inconsiderately gets himself knocked off. Just *informing* all these different people takes a lot of time. Imagine having to call the Police Commissioner, *and* the Chief of Detectives, *and* the District Commander of the Detective Division, *and* Homicide, *and* the Squad and Precinct Commanding Officers of the precinct where the body was found, *and* the Medical Examiner, *and* the District Attorney, *and* the Telegraph, Telephone and Teletype Bureau at Headquarters, *and* the Police Laboratory, not to mention the police photographers and stenographers—the list alone is longer than the average laundry list, and just try phoning in a dirty shirt to the local laundryman. All that vast machinery of law enforcement ground into immediate action the moment it was discovered that Albert Weinberg had a hole in his

chest; all those oiled gears smoothly meshed and rotated
in the cause of justice; all those relentless preventers of
crime and pursuers of criminals called upon their enormous reservoir of physical courage and stamina, their
mental acumen, their experience, intelligence, their *bril-
liance* even—and all in an attempt to discover who had
shot and killed the man who once upon a time had beat
up a little old lady for the sum of seventeen dollars and
thirty-four cents.

Actually, most of the physical courage and stamina,
the mental acumen, the experience, intelligence and bril-
liance was being expended by Detectives Meyer Meyer
and Cotton Hawes of the 87th Squad; Carella (who had
discovered the corpse) being elsewhere occupied. Meyer
and Hawes did not have much trouble taking apart the
apartment; whoever killed Weinberg had already done a
very good job of that. They decided after a thorough
search of the place that Brown's surmise was a correct
one. The killer had been after Weinberg's pieces of the
photograph, and had apparently been successful in finding
them. Meyer and Hawes questioned all of the tenants
in the building and discovered that three of them had
heard a very loud noise shortly after midnight. None of
these people thought it either necessary or advisable to
call the police. In this neighborhood, policemen were not
exactly looked upon as benefactors of the people, and
besides the sounds of gunfire were somewhat common-
place, day *or* night. So both detectives went back to the
squadroom to consult the timetable Irving Krutch had so
thoughtfully typed up for Steve Carella:

6:00 P.M.	-- ARRIVED HOME FROM WORK. TALKED TO DOORMAN DOWNSTAIRS ABOUT FINE WEATHER.
6:05 P.M.	-- ENTERED APARTMENT. CALLED SUZANNE ENDICOTT, REMINDED HER OF OUR DATE.
6:15 P.M.	-- RAN BATH, MIXED MARTINIS, CAUGHT LAST PART OF SIX O'CLOCK NEWS ON TELEVISION WHILE WAIT-ING FOR TUB TO FILL.
6:30 P.M. to 7:30 P.M.	-- BATHED, SHAVED, DRESSED, MIXED ANOTHER PITCHER-FUL OF MARTINIS.
7:30 P.M.	-- SUZIE ARRIVED AT APARTMENT. WE EACH HAD TWO MARTINIS.

8:00 P.M.   -- ARTHUR BROWN CALLED TO ADVISE ME OF NEW DEVEL-
              OPMENTS ON CASE.

8:25 P.M.   -- CALLED DOWNSTAIRS, ASKED DOORMAN TO GET ME A
              TAXICAB.

8:30 P.M.   -- SUZIE AND I WENT DOWNSTAIRS, TAXI WAITING,
              TOOK TAXI TO THE RAM'S HEAD, 777 JEFFERSON
              AVENUE. (RESERVATION FOR 8:45 P.M. MADE BY
              MY SECRETARY, DONNA HOGAN, EARLIER IN DAY.)

8:45 P.M.)   -- DINNER AT THE RAM'S HEAD. HEADWAITER MAURICE
to
10:30 P.M.)   SUGGESTED THE CHATEAU BOUSCAUT '64.

10:30 P.M.)   -- WALKED UP HALL AVENUE LOOKING IN SHOP WINDOWS,
to
11:30 P.M.)   AND FINALLY HAILED TAXI.

11:45 P.M.   -- TAXI DROPPED US AT APARTMENT. CAME UPSTAIRS.
              I HAD A COGNAC, SUZIE HAD A CREME DE MENTHE ON
              THE ROCKS. WATCHED JOHNNY CARSON FOR APPROXI-
              MATELY A HALF-HOUR. BUDDY HACKETT GUEST STAR.

12:15 A.M.   -- WENT TO BED.

3:15 A.M.   -- AWAKENED BY KNOCKING ON DOOR. DETECTIVE STEVE
              CARELLA IN HALLWAY OUTSIDE.

3:15 A.M.)   -- TALKED TO DETECTIVE CARELLA.
to
3:25 A.M.)

3:25 A.M.   -- TYPED TIMETABLE FOR DETECTIVE CARELLA.

3:30 A.M.   -- DETECTIVE CARELLA LEFT. WENT BACK TO BED.

The day doorman outside Krutch's apartment building
corroborated that Krutch had come home from work at
about 6 P.M., and that they had had a brief discussion
about the wonderful weather, so different from last June's
weather, when the city was sweltering in the grip of a
ninety-degree heat wave. He put Meyer and Hawes in
touch with the night doorman who stated that Krutch
had called down for a taxi at approximately eight-thirty,
and had left the building with a young lady shortly thereafter. He had personally given Krutch's destination to the
cab driver: The Ram's Head at 777 Jefferson Avenue.
He further reported that Krutch and the young lady had
come back to the apartment shortly before midnight and
that he had not seen either of them leaving again at any
time during his tour of duty, which ended at 8 A.M., Meyer
and Hawes went over the building's entrances very care-

fully, though, and discovered that anyone who chose not to be seen by either the doorman or the elevator operator had only to take the service steps down to the basement and leave the building through the side-street exit door, where the garbage cans were stacked.

The reservations book for The Ram's Head noted a reservation for "Irving Krutch, 2" at 8:45 P.M. on the night Albert Weinberg was murdered. The headwaiter, a man named Maurice Duchene recalled Mr. Krutch and a young lady being there, and also recalled recommending the Chateau Bouscaut '64 to them. He said that Mr. Krutch had ordered a bottle and had commented that the wine was delicious. Mr. Krutch had tipped him three dollars when he left the restaurant at about ten-thirty.

A call to the local affiliate of the National Broadcasting Company ascertained the fact that one of Johnny Carson's guests that night had been Buddy Hackett and that he had come on almost immediately after the monologue, sometime before midnight.

There was nothing left to do but talk to Suzanne Endicott.

Ask any cop whom he would rather interview, an eighty-year-old lady with varicose veins or a twenty-two-year-old blonde wearing a see-through blouse, just ask any cop.

Suzanne Endicott worked in a swinging boutique called The Nickel Bag, and she was wearing a leather mini-skirt and a blouse through which her breasts were clearly visible. Her attire was very disconcerting, especially to policemen who were rather more used to eighty-year-old ladies with varicose veins. Detective Meyer Meyer was a married man. Cotton Hawes was a single man, but he, too, seemed to be having difficulty concentrating on the questions. He kept thinking he should ask Suzanne Endicott to go to a movie with him. Or something. The shop was thronged with young girls similarly though not identically dressed, mini-skirts and tights, headbands and shiny blouses, a veritable aviary of chirping young birds —Meyer Meyer hadn't even enjoyed the Hitchcock film. Suzanne Endicott fluttered here and there, helping this young lady with a pants suit, that one with a crocheted dress, the next with a sequined vest. Between flutterings and chirpings and quick glimpses of nipples and thighs, the detectives tried to ask their questions.

"You want to tell us exactly what happened that night?" Meyer asked.

"Oh, sure, I'd be happy to," Suzie said. She had the faintest trace of a Southern accent in her speech, Hawes noticed.

"Where are you from originally?" he asked, thinking to put her at ease, and also thinking he would definitely ask her to go to a movie or something.

"Oh my, does my accent still show?" Suzie said.

"Just a little," Hawes said, and tried a gentle understanding smile which did not seem appropriate to his massive height, nor his fiery red mane, nor the white streak in the hair over his left temple, the result of a knifing many years back.

"I'm from Georgia," she said. "The Peach State."

"It must be lovely down there in Georgia," Hawes said.

"Oh yes, just lovely," Suzie said. "Excuse me, just one teeny little minute, won't you?" she said, and dashed off to where a striking brunette was coming out of one of the dressing rooms. The brunette had on bright red velvet hip-huggers. Hawes thought he might go over and ask *her* to go to a movie or something.

"Ie feel as if I'm backstage at the Folies-Bergère," Meyer whispered.

"Have you ever *been* backstage at the Folies-Bergère?" Hawes whispered back.

"No, but I'm sure it's just like this."

"Better," Hawes said.

"Have *you* ever been?"

"Never."

"Well, here I am, back again," Suzie said, and smiled, and tossed her long blond hair and added, "I think they were a bit too snug, don't you?"

"What's that?" Meyer said.

"The pants she had on."

"Oh, sure, a little too snug," Meyer said. "Miss Endicott, about the night Weinberg was killed . . ."

"Oh, yes, that was just dreadful, wasn't it?" Suzie said.

"Yes, it was," Hawes said gently and tenderly.

"Although I understand he was a criminal. Weinberg, I mean."

"Who told you that?"

"Irving did. *Was* he a criminal?"

"He paid his debt to society," Hawes said tenderly and gently.

"Oh, yes, I suppose he did," Suzie answered. "But still."

"In any event," Meyer said, passing a hand over his bald pate and rolling his china-blue eyes, "he *was* killed, and we're conducting an investigation into his murder, and we'd like very much to ask you some questions about that night, if it's not too much trouble, Miss Endicott."

"Oh, it's no trouble at all," Suzie said. "Would you p'ease excuse me for just one teeny minute?" she said, and went over to the cash register where a leggy redhead was standing with several sweaters in her arms, waiting to pay for them.

"We'll *never* get out of this joint," Meyer said.

"That wouldn't be too bad," Hawes said.

"For *you,* maybe it wouldn't be too bad. For *me,* if I don't get home in time for dinner, Sarah'll kill me."

"Why don't you run on along then?" Hawes said, and grinned. "I think I can handle this alone."

"Oh, I'm sure you can," Meyer said. "Trouble is, you see, we're supposed to find out who killed Weinberg. That's the trouble, you see."

"Well, here I am back again," Suzie said, and smiled, and tossed her long blond hair. "I've asked Michelle to spell me, so I don't think we'll be interrupted again."

"That's very kind of you, Suzie," Hawes said.

"Oh, not at all," she answered, and smiled again.

"About that night . . ."

"Yes," she said, alert, and responsive, and eager to co-operate. "What would you like to know?"

"First, what time did you get to Irving Krutch's apartment?"

"It must have been about seven-thirty," Suzie said.

"How long have you known Mr. Krutch?" Hawes said.

"We've practically been living together for four years," Suzie answered, her big brown eyes opened wide.

"Oh," Hawes said.

"Yes."

"I see."

"We have separate apartments, of course."

"Of course."

Meyer cleared his throat. "What . . . uh . . . what was I saying?" he said, turning to Hawes.

"Time she got there," Hawes said.

"Oh yes. Seven-thirty, is that right?"

"That's right," Suzie said.

"And what did you do when you got there?"

"Irving gave me a martini. Two martinis, in fact. I love martinis. Don't you just adore martinis?" she asked Hawes.

"Mmm," Hawes said.

"Were there any visitors while you were there?"

"None."

"Any phone calls?"

"Yes."

"Would you happen to know from whom?"

"From a detective. Irving seemed very happy when he hung up."

"Are you engaged or something?" Hawes asked. "Is that it?"

"To be married, do you mean?"

"Yes, to be married."

"Oh, no, don't be silly," Suzie said.

Meyer cleared his throat again. "What time did you *leave* the apartment?" he asked.

"About eight-thirty. I think it was eight-thirty. It could have been a teeny bit earlier or a teeny bit later. But I think it was *around* eight-thirty."

"And where did you go?"

"To The Ram's Head." She smiled up at Hawes. "That's a restaurant. Have you ever been there?"

"No. No, I haven't."

"It's very nice."

"What time did you leave the restaurant, Miss Endicott?"

"About ten-thirty. Again, as I said, it might have been a teeny bit . . ."

"Yes, but it was *around* ten-thirty."

"Yes."

"And then what did you do?"

"We went for a walk on Hall Avenue, and looked in all the store windows. We saw some marvelous lounging pajamas in Kilkenny's. Italian, I thing they were. Just, oh so colorful."

"How long did you walk on Hall Avenue?"

"An hour or so? I guess it was an hour or so."

"And then what did you do?"

"We went back to Irving's apartment. What we do, you see, is we either go to Irving's apartment or to my apartment. I live downtown in The Quarter," she said, looking up at Hawes. "Do you know Chelsea Street?"

"Yes, I do," Hawes said.

"12½ Chelsea Street," she said, "apartment 6B. That's because of hard luck."

"What is?"

"The 12½. It should be 13, but the owner of the building is superstitious."

"Yes, there are lots of buildings in the city like that," Hawes said.

"Lots of buildings don't even have a thirteenth *floor*," Suzie said. "That is, they *have* a thirteenth floor, but it's called the *fourteenth* floor."

"Yes, I know."

"12½ Chelsea Street," she said, "apartment 6B, Hampton 4-8100." She paused. "That's my telephone number."

"So you went back to Mr. Krutch's apartment at about eleven-thirty," Meyer said, "and then what did you do?"

"We watched television for a while. Buddy Hackett was on. He's a scream. Don't you just adore Buddy Hackett?" she said, looking up at Hawes.

"I adore him, yes," Hawes said, and Meyer gave him a peculiar look. "He's very comical," Hawes said, ignoring the look.

"He's just adorable," Suzie said.

"What did you do after watching television?" Meyer said.

"We made love," Suzie said.

Meyer cleared his throat.

"Twice," Suzie added.

Meyer cleared his throat again.

"Then we went to sleep," she said, "and in the middle of the night this Italian detective knocked on the door and started asking all sorts of questions about where we were and what we were doing. Is he allowed to do something like that, come around in the middle of the night, and bang on the door, and ask dumb questions?"

"Yes, he is," Hawes said.

"I think that's awful," Suzie said. "Don't you think that's awful?" she asked Hawes.

"Well, it's a job," Hawes said, and smiled weakly, and tried to avoid Meyer's glance again.

"Did either of you leave the apartment at any time between 11:30 and 3 A.M.?" Meyer asked.

"Oh, no. I told you. First we watched television, and then we made love, and then we went to sleep."

"You were there all the time?"

"Yes."

"Both of you."

"Yes."

"Mr. Krutch didn't leave the apartment at all."

"No."

"If you were asleep, how do you know whether he left or not?"

"Well, we didn't go to sleep until about maybe two o'clock. Things take *time*, you know."

"You were awake until 2 A.M.?"

"Yes."

"And Mr. Krutch did not leave the apartment?"

"No."

"Did he leave the bedroom?"

"No."

"Not at any time during the night?"

"Not at any time during the night."

"Okay," Meyer said. "You got anything else, Cotton?"

"Is that your name?" Suzie asked. "I had an uncle named Cotton."

"That's my name," Hawes said.

"After Cotton Mather?"

"That's right."

"Isn't that a coincidence?" Suzie said. "I think that's a marvelous coincidence."

"You got anything else to ask?" Meyer said again.

"Well . . . yes," Hawes said, and looked at Meyer.

"I'll wait for you outside," Meyer said.

"Okay," Hawes said.

He watched as Meyer picked his way through the milling girls in the shop, watched as Meyer opened the front door and stepped out onto the sidewalk.

"I have only one further question, Suzie," he said.

"Yes, what's that?"

"Would you like to go to a movie with me? Or something?"

"Oh, no," Suzie said. "Irving wouldn't like that." She smiled and looked up at him with her big brown eyes. "I'm terribly sorry," she said, "really I am, but Irving simply wouldn't like that at all."

"Well, uh, thanks a lot for your co-operation, Miss Endicott," Hawes said. "Thank you very much, I'm sorry we—uh—broke into your day this way, thanks a lot."

"Not at all," Suzie said, and rushed off to another beautiful brunette who was emerging from yet another dressing room. Hawes looked at the brunette, decided not to risk further rejection, and went outside to where Meyer was waiting on the sidewalk.

"Did you score?" Meyer asked.

"Nope."

"How come? I thought it was a sure thing."

"So did I. I guess she thinks Krutch is just adorable."

"I think *you're* just adorable," Meyer said.

"Up yours," Hawes answered, and both men went back to the squadroom. Hawes typed up the report and then went out to talk to a grocery store owner who had a complaint about people stealing bottles of milk from boxes stacked up in back of the store, this in the wee hours of the morning before the store was opened for business. Meyer went to talk to an assault victim and to show him some mug shots for possible identification. They had worked long and hard on the Weinberg Case, yeah, and it was now in the Open File, pending further developments.

Meanwhile, on the ferry to Bethtown, two other cops were working very hard at sniffing the mild June breezes that blew in off the River Harb. Coatless, hatless, Carella and Brown stood at the railing and watched Isola's receding skyline, watched too the busy traffic on the river, tugboats and ocean liners, a squadron of Navy destroyers, barges and scows, each of them tooting and chugging and sounding bells and sending up steam and leaving a boiling, frothy wake behind.

"This is still the cheapest date in the city," Brown said. "Five cents for a forty-five minute boat ride—who can beat it?"

"I wish *I* had a nickel for all the times I rode this ferry with Teddy, before we were married," Carella said.

"Caroline used to love it," Brown said. "She never wanted to sit inside, winter or summer. We always stood here on the bow, even if it meant freezing our asses off."

"The poor man's ocean cruise," Carella said.

"Moonlight and sea breezes . . ."

"Concertina playing . . ."

"Tugboats honking . . ."

"Sounds like a Warner Brothers movie."

"I sometimes thought it *was,*" Brown said wistfully. "There were lots of places I couldn't go in this city, Steve, either because I couldn't afford them or because it was made plain to me I wasn't wanted in them. On the Bethtown ferry, though, I could be the hero of the movie. I could take my girl out on the bow and we could feel the wind on our faces, and I could kiss her like a colored Humphrey Bogart. I love this goddamn ferry, I really do."

"Yeah," Carella said, and nodded.

"Sure," Robert Coombs said, "I used to have a piece of that picture."

"*Used* to have?" Brown asked.

"*Used* to have, correct," Coombs said, and spat on the sidewalk in front of the hot-dog stand. He was a man of about sixty, with a weather-beaten face, spikes of yellow-white hair sticking up out of his skull like withered stalks of corn, an altogether grizzled look about him as he sat on one of the stools in front of his establishment (Bob's Roadside) and talked to the two detectives. The hot-dog stand was on Route 24, off the beaten path; it was unlikely that a dozen automobiles passed the place on any given day, in either direction.

"Where'd you get it?" Carella asked.

"Petey Ryan give it to me before the holdup," Coombs said. His eyes were a pale blue, fringed with blond lashes, overhung with blond-white brows. His teeth were the color of his brows. He spat again on the sidewalk. Brown wondered what it was like to eat food prepared at Bob's Roadside.

"Why'd Ryan give it to you?" Carella asked.

"We was good friends," Coombs said.

"Tell us all about it," Brown suggested.

"What for? I already told you I ain't got the picture no more."

"Where is it now?"

"Christ knows," Coombs said, and shrugged, and spat.

"How long before the holdup?" Carella said.

"How long *what?*"

"When he gave you the picture."

"Three days."

"Petey came to you . . ."

"Correct."

"And handed you a piece of a snapshot . . ."

"Correct."

"And said what?"

"Said I should hang onto it till after the hit."

"And then what?"

"Then he'd come collect it from me."

"Did he say why?"

"In case he got busted."

"He didn't want to have the picture on him if the police caught him, is that it?"

"Correct."

"What did you think about all that?" Brown asked.

"What should I think? A good friend asks me to do a favor, I do it. What was there to think?"

"Did you have any idea what the picture meant?"

"Sure."

"What did it mean?"

"It showed where they was ditching the loot. You think I'm a dope?"

"Did Petey say how many pieces there were in the complete photograph?"

"Nope."

"Just told you to hang onto this little piece of it until he came to collect it?"

"Correct."

"Okay, where's the piece now?"

"I threw it in the garbage," Coombs said.

"Why?"

"Petey got killed. Cinch he wasn't going to come back for the piece, so I thrown it out."

"Even though you knew it was part of a bigger picture? A picture that showed where they were dropping the N.S.L.A. loot?"

"Correct."

"When did you throw it out?"

"Day after the hit. Soon as I read in the paper that Petey got killed."

"You were in a pretty big hurry to get rid of it, huh?"

"A pretty big hurry, correct."

"Why?"

"I didn't want to get hooked into the holdup. I figured if the picture was hot, I didn't want no part of it."

"But you accepted it from Petey to begin with, didn't you?"

"Correct."

"Even though you knew it showed where they planned to hide the proceeds of a robbery."

"I only *guessed* that. I didn't know for sure."

"When did you find out for sure?"

"Well, I *still* don't know for sure."

"But you became sufficiently alarmed *after* the robbery to throw away the scrap Petey had given you."

"Correct."

"This was six years ago, right, Mr. Coombs?"

"Correct."

"You threw it in the garbage."

"In the garbage, correct."

"Where was the garbage?"

"Where was the *what?*"

"The garbage."

"In the back."

"Out back there?"

"Correct."

"You want to come back there with us, and show us where you threw it in the garbage?"

"Sure," Coombs said, and got off the stool, and spat, and then led them around to the rear side of the hot-dog stand. "Right there," he said, pointing. "In one of them garbage cans."

"You carried that little tiny piece of the photograph out back here, and you lifted the lid of the garbage can and dropped it in, is that right?"

"Correct."

"Show us how you did it," Brown said.

Coombs looked at him curiously. Then he shrugged, pinched an imaginary photograph segment between his thumb and forefinger, carried it to the nearest garbage can, lifted the lid, deposited the non-existent scrap inside the can, covered the can, turned to the cops, and said, "Like that. That's how I done it."

"You're lying," Brown said flatly.

Neither of the two detectives, of course, knew whether or not Coombs was lying, nor had their little charade with the garbage can proved a damn thing. But public relations has a lot to do with criminal investigation and detection. There is not a red-blooded citizen of the U.S. of A. who does not know through constant exposure to television programs and motion pictures that cops are always asking trick questions and doing trick things to trap a person in a lie. Coombs had seen his share of movies and television shows, and he knew now, knew with heart-stopping, face-blanching, teeth-jarring certainty that he had done something wrong when he walked over to the garbage can, and lifted the lid, and dropped in the imaginary photo scrap, something that had instantly told these two shrewd investigators that he was lying.

"Lying?" he said. "Me? Lying?" He tried to spit again, but his throat muscles wouldn't respond, and he almost choked, and then began coughing violently.

"You want to come along with us?" Carella said, sternly and pompously, and in his most legal-sounding voice.

"Wh . . . wh . . . wh . . .?" Coombs said, and coughed again, his face turning purple, and then put one hand flat against the rear wall of the hot-dog stand, head bent, and leaned against it, and tried to catch his breath and recover his wits. They had him cold, he knew, but he couldn't figure what the charge would be, and he tried to buy time now while the big black cop reached into his back pocket and pulled out a pair of handcuffs with vicious-looking saw-toothed edges—oh Jesus, Coombs thought, I am busted. But for what?

"What's the crime," he said, "the charge," he said, "what's the, what's the, what did I do?"

"You know what you did, Mr. Coombs," Carella said, coldly. "You destroyed evidence of a crime."

"That a felony," Brown said, lying.

"Section·812 of the Penal Law," Carella said.

"Look, I . . ."

"Come along, Mr. Coombs," Brown said, and held out the handcuffs.

"What if I . . . what if I hadn't thrown out the thing, the picture?" Coombs asked.

"Did you?"

"I didn't. I got it. I'll give it to you. Jesus, I'll give it to you."

"Get it," Brown said.

A ferryboat is a good place for speculation. It is also a good place for listening. So on the way back to Isola, Carella and Brown each did a little speculating and a little listening.

"Four guys in the holdup," Brown said. "Carmine Bonamico, who masterminded the job . . ."

"Some mastermind," Carella said.

"Jerry Stein, who drove the getaway heap, and two guns named Lou D'Amore and Pete Ryan. Four altogether."

"So?"

"So figure it out. Pete Ryan gave one piece of the snapshot to his aunt Dorothea McNally and another piece to his good old pal Robert Coombs . . ."

"Of Bob's Famous Roadside Emporium," Carella said.

"Correct," Brown said. "Which means, using a method known as arithmetical deduction, that Ryan was at one time in possession of *two* pieces of the snapshot."

"Correct," Carella said.

"Is it not reasonable to assume, therefore, that *each* member of the gang was *likewise* in possession of two pieces of the snapshot?"

"It is reasonable, but not necessarily exclusive," Carella said.

"How do you mean, Holmes?"

"Elementary. You are assuming there are only *eight* pieces of the full photograph. However, using other multiples of four, we can equally reason that there are twelve pieces, or sixteen pieces, or indeed . . ."

"My guess is eight," Brown said.

"Why the magic number eight?"

"If you were planning a heist, would you go cutting a picture into twelve parts? Or sixteen?"

"Or twenty?" Carella said.

"*Would* you?"

"I think it's a goofy idea to begin with," Carella said. "I wouldn't cut up a photograph at *all*."

"My guess is eight. Four guys, two pieces each. We've now got six of them. My guess is we'll find number seven in Gerry Ferguson's safe. That'll leave only one

piece to go. One, baby. One more piece and we're home free."

As Robert Burns, that sage Scottish poet once remarked, however, the best laid plans . . .

That afternoon, they went down to the Ferguson Gallery with a warrant obliging Geraldine Ferguson to open her safe. And though they searched it from top to bottom and found a lot of goodies in it, none of which were related to any crime, they did *not* find another piece of the photograph. By the end of that Monday, they still had only six pieces.

Six.

Count 'em.

Six.

As they studied these assembled pieces in the midnight silence of the squadroom, something struck them as being terribly wrong. There was no sky in the picture. And because there was no sky, neither was there an up nor a down, a top nor a bottom. They were looking at a landscape without perspective, and it made no sense.

10

THE NYLON stocking was wrapped tightly around her throat, embedded in the soft flesh of her neck. Her eyes were bulging, and she lay grotesque in death upon the turquoise-colored rug in her bedroom, wearing a baby-doll nightgown and bikini panties, the bedsheets trailing off the bed and tangled in one twisted leg.

Geraldine Ferguson would never again swear in Italian, never again proposition married spades, never again charge exorbitant prices for a painting or a piece of sculpture. Geraldine Ferguson lay robbed of life in a posture as angularly absurd as the geometric designs that had shrieked from the walls of her gallery, death silent and shrill in that turquoise-matted sanctuary, the bedroom a bedlam around her, a tired reprise of the havoc wreaked in the rooms of Donald Renninger and Albert Weinberg, the searcher run amok, the quest for seven hundred and fifty G's reaching a climax of desperation. The police had not found what they'd wanted in Gerry's safe, and they wondered now if whoever had demolished Gerry's apartment and strangled her into the bargain had had any better luck than they.

Arthur Brown went out into the hallway and, oddly, wondered if Gerry had ever roller-skated on a city sidewalk.

They picked up Bramley Kahn in a gay bar that night. He was wearing a brocade Nehru jacket over white linen hip-huggers. His hand was resting on the shoulder of a curly-haired young man in a black leather jacket. A sculpted gold ring set with a gray freshwater pearl was on Kahn's left pinky.

He was slightly drunk, and decidedly campy, and he seemed surprised to see the police. Everywhere around him, men danced with men, men whispered to men, men embraced men, but Kahn was nonetheless surprised to see the police because this was the most permissive city in the world, where private homosexual clubs could expressly prohibit policemen from entering (unless of course they, too, were members) and where everyone looked the other way unless a six-year-old boy was being buggered by a flying queen in a dark alley. This was just a run-of-the-mill gay bar, never any trouble here, never any strident jealous arguments, never anything more than consenting adults quietly doing their thing—Kahn was very surprised to see the police.

He was even more surprised to learn that Geraldine Ferguson was dead.

He kept telling the police how surprised he was.

This was a Tuesday, he kept telling the police, and Tuesday was normally Gerry's day off; she took Tuesdays, he took Wednesdays. He had not expected to see her at the gallery and was not surprised when she did not show up for work. He had closed the gallery at six, had gone for a quiet dinner with a close friend, and then had come down here to The Quarter for a nightcap before turning in. Arthur Brown asked him if he would mind coming uptown to the squadroom, and Kahn said he could see no objection to that, though perhaps he had better first consult his lawyer. Brown said he was entitled to a lawyer, and in fact didn't have to answer any questions at all if he didn't want to, lawyer or no lawyer, and then went into the whole Miranda-Escobedo bit, advising Kahn of his rights while Kahn listened intently, and then decided that he had *better* call his lawyer and have him come up to the squadroom to be present during the interrogation, murder being a somewhat serious occurrence, even in a city as permissive as this one.

The lawyer was a man named Anatole Petitpas, and he asked Brown to do the whole Miranda-Escobedo song and dance one more time for the benefit of the people in the cheaper seats. Brown patiently explained Kahn's rights to him again, and Kahn said that he understood everything, and Petitpas seemed satisfied that all was be-

ing conducted in a proper legal manner, and then he
signaled to the detectives that it was now all right to ask
his client whatever questions they chose to ask. There
were four detectives standing in a loose circle around
Kahn, but their weight of numbers was offset by the
presence of Petitpas, who could be counted on to leap
into the fray if ever the questioning got too rough. This
was murder they were fooling around with here, and nobody was taking any chances.

They asked all the routine questions (almost putting
even themselves to sleep) such as WHERE WERE YOU
AT 2 A.M. LAST NIGHT? (the time established by the
M.E. as the probable time of Gerry's death) and WHO
WAS WITH YOU? and WHERE DID YOU GO? and
WERE YOU SEEN BY ANYONE?, all the usual police
crap, the questions coming alternately from Brown, Carella, Meyer, and Hawes working smoothly and efficient-
ly as a team. And then finally they got back to the photograph, everything always got back to the photograph because it was obvious to each of the cops in that squadroom that four people had been killed so far and that all
of them had been in possession of a piece or pieces of a
picture showing the location of the N.S.L.A. loot, and if
a motive were any more evident than that, each of them
would have tripped over it with his big flat feet.

"When I talked to you at the gallery Saturday," Brown
said, "you told me Gerry Ferguson was in possession of
a certain piece of a photograph. When you said this, were
you . . ."

"Just a second," Petitpas interrupted. "Have you talked
to my client before this?"

"I talked to him, yes."

"Did you advise him of his rights?"

"I was conducting a field investigation," Brown said
wearily.

"He didn't tell me he was a cop," Kahn said.

"Is that true?" Petitpas asked.

"It's true."

"It may be significant."

"Not necessarily," Brown said, and smiled. The other
detectives smiled with him. They were thinking of thou-
sands of social agency reports in triplicate where, for
example, a young man would be described as having been
arrested at the age of fourteen for possession of nar-
cotics, at sixteen for possession with intent to sell, and
at eighteen for smuggling in twelve kilos of heroin in a

brown paper bag, all of which damning criminal history
would be followed by the words, typewritten in upper
case,   NOT NECESSARILY SIGNIFICANT.

"Go on," Petitpas said.

"I wanted to ask your client whether he knew for certain that Miss Ferguson had a piece of that photograph."

"I knew for certain," Kahn said.

"Miss Ferguson told us the piece was in the gallery
safe," Carella said. "Was that your impression as well?"

"It was my impression."

"As you know, however, when we opened the safe, we
did not find the photograph."

"I know that."

"Where did you think it was then?" Hawes asked.

"I don't understand your question."

"When you found out it wasn't in the safe, when we
opened the safe yesterday and the picture wasn't in it,
where did you think it might be?"

"I had no idea."

"Did you think it was in Miss Ferguson's apartment?"
Meyer asked.

"He has already told you he had no idea where it was,"
Petitpas said. "You're asking him to speculate . . ."

"Let's save it for the courtroom, counselor," Carella
said. "There's nothing out of line here so far, and you
know it. A woman's been killed. If your client can satisfy
us on certain points, he'll walk out of here in ten minutes.
If not . . ."

"Yes, Mr. Canella?"

"Carella. If not, I think you're as well aware of the
possibilities as we are."

"Are you threatening him with a murder charge?"

"Did anyone mention a murder charge?"

"The implication was clear."

"So was Detective Meyer's question. Mr. Kahn, did
you or did you not think the photograph might be in Miss
Ferguson's apartment?"

"May I answer that?" Kahn asked his lawyer.

"Yes, go ahead, go ahead," Petitpas said, annoyed.

"I guess I thought it could have been there, yes."

"Did you go there looking for it?" Brown asked.

"That's *it*, I'm afraid," Petitpas said. "I feel I must
advise my client at this point that it would not be to his
benefit to answer any further questions."

"Do you want us to book him, counselor, is that it?"

"You may do as you wish. I know I don't have to re- mind you that murder is a serious . . ."

"Oh, man, what bullshit," Brown said. "Why don't you just play ball with us, Petitpas? Has your man got some- thing to hide?'

"I've got nothing to hide, Anatole," Kahn said.

"Then let him answer the goddamn questions," Carella said.

"I can answer the questions," Kahn said, and looked at Petitpas.

"Very well, go ahead," Petitpas said.

"I didn't kill her, Anatole."

"Go ahead, go ahead."

"I really didn't. I have nothing to hide."

"Okay, counselor?"

"I have already indicated that he may answer your questions."

"Thank you. Did you go to Gerry Ferguson's apart- ment last night?"

"No."

"Or any time yesterday?"

"No."

"Did you see her yesterday?"

"Yes, at the gallery. I left before she did. This was sometime after you'd opened the safe."

"Sometime after you knew the picture wasn't in the safe?"

"That's right, yes."

"And sometime after you thought it might be in Miss Ferguson's apartment?'

"Yes."

"Let's talk about the list, Mr. Kahn."

"What?"

"The list."

"What list?"

"The torn list of names you keep in a little cashbox in the bottom drawer of your office desk."

"I . . . I don't know what you mean," Kahn said.

"Four people on that list have already been killed, Mr. Kahn."

"What list does he mean, Bram?" Petitpas asked.

"I don't know."

"It's a list of names, Mr. Petitpas," Brown said, "presumably of people who possess or once possessed portions of a photograph alleging to show the location of certain monies stolen from the National Savings &

Loan Association six years ago. Does that clearly identify the nature of the list, Mr. Kahn?"

Petitpas stared at his client. Kahn stared back at him.

"Well, answer it," Petitpas said.

"It clearly identifies the nature of the list, yes," Kahn
said.

"Then the list *does* exist?"

"It exists."

"And a torn portion of it is indeed in your cashbox?"

"It is, yes, but how . . .?"

"Never mind how. Where'd you get that list?"

"Gerry gave it to me for safekeeping."

"Where'd *she* get it?"

"I don't know."

"Mr. Kahn, try to help us," Meyer said gently.

"I didn't kill her," Kahn said.

"Somebody did," Carella said.

"It wasn't me."

"We're not suggesting it was."

"All right. As long as you know."

"Who gave her the list?"

"Carmine."

"Bonamico?"

"Yes. Carmine Bonamico. He gave half of the list to
his wife, and half to Geraldine."

"Why Geraldine?"

"They were having a thing."

"They were lovers?"

"Yes."

"Did he also give her a piece of the photograph?"

"No. She got that from her brother-in-law, Lou
D'Amore. There were four men on the holdup. Bonamico
cut the picture into eight parts, a wiggly line across the
middle horizontally, three wiggly lines vertically, eight
pieces in all. He gave two pieces to each of the men,
and kept two for himself. He asked the men to distribute
the pieces to people they could trust. It was an insurance
policy, so to speak. The beneficiaries were the people
who held sections of the photograph. The trustees were
Alice Bonamico and Gerry Ferguson, the only two people
who could put together the list and collect the photograph
segments and uncover the loot."

"Who told you all this?"

"Gerry."

"How'd she know?"

"Pillow talk. Bonamico told her everything. I don't

think his wife knew who had the other half of the list.
But Gerry sure as hell knew."

"So Gerry was in possession of half of the list as well
as one piece of the photograph."

"Yes."

"Why didn't she put the list together and go after the
other pieces?"

"She tried to."

"What stopped her?"

"Alice." Kahn paused. "Well, after all, would *your* wife
co-operate with your mistress?"

"I don't have a mistress," Carella said.

"Here's a typewritten copy of the list," Brown said.
"Take a look at it."

"Is it all right to look at it?" Kahn asked his lawyer.

"Yes," Petitpas said. He turned to the police stenographer and said. "Let the record indicate that Mr. Kahn
is being shown a list with such-and-such names on it;
record all the names as they appear on the list."

"May I see the list?" the stenographer asked.

Brown handed it to him. The stenographer studied it,
noted the names, and then handed it back to Brown.

"All right, Mr. Kahn, would you now please look at
this list?"

Kahn accepted the list.

ALBERT WEINBERG

DONALD RENNINGER

EUGENE E. EHRBACH

ALICE BONAMICO

GERALDINE FERGUSON

DOROTHEA MCNALLY

ROBERT COOMBS

"I've looked at it," he said, and handed it back to
Brown.

"Which of those names are familiar to you?"

"Only three of them."

"Which?"

"Gerry, of course, Alice Bonamico, and Donald Renninger. He's the other person who got a piece of the picture from Lou D'Amore."

"How come?"

"They were cellmates at Caramoor. In fact, Lou
mailed the piece to him there. He was still behind bars
at the time of the robbery."

"What about these other names?"

"I don't know any of them."

"Robert Coombs?"

"Don't know him."

"His name was on the half of the list you had in your possession. Didn't you ever try to contact him?"

"Gerry may have. I didn't."

"You weren't at all curious about him, is that right?"

"Oh, I was *curious,* I suppose, but not curious enough to go all the way out to . . ." Kahn suddenly stopped.

"Out to where, Mr. Kahn?"

"All right, Bethtown. I *did* go to see him. He wouldn't give up the piece. I offered him twelve hundred dollars for it, but he wouldn't give it up."

"How about some of these other names? Did you ever try to contact any of them?"

"How could I? I only had half the list."

"There are only seven names on this list, Mr. Kahn."

"Yes, I noticed that."

"You said the picture had been divided into eight pieces."

"That's what Gerry told me."

"Who's got the eighth piece?"

"I don't know."

"How about this first name on the list, Mr. Kahn? Albert Weinberg? Are you trying to say you've never heard of him?"

"Never."

"Don't you read the newspapers?"

"Oh, you mean his murder. Yes, of course, I read about his murder. I thought you were referring . . ."

"Yes?"

"To my having some knowledge of him *before* then."

"Did you kill Albert Weinberg?"

"Just a second, Mr. Brown . . ."

"It's all right, Anatole," Kahn said. "No, I did *not* kill him, Mr. Brown. In fact, before the night of his murder, I didn't even know he *existed.*"

"I see," Brown said. "Even though he'd been in the gallery several times to inquire about the photograph?"

"Yes, but always using an assumed name."

"I see."

"I had nothing to do with either murder."

"Did you have anything to do with beating me up?"

"I should say not!"

"Where were you at the time?"

"Home in bed!"

"When?"

"The night you were beat up."

"How do you know it happened at night?"

"Just a second, Mr. Brown . . ."

"No, it's all right, Anatole," Kahn said. "Gerry told me."

"Who told Gerry?"

"Why, *you* I would guess."

"No, I didn't tell her anything about it."

"Then she must have known some other way. Maybe she was involved in it. Maybe she hired someone to go to your hotel . . ."

"How do you know that's where it happened?"

"She . . . she said so."

"She said I'd been attacked by two men in my hotel room?"

"Yes, she told me about it the next day."

"She couldn't have told you there were *two* men, Mr. Kahn, because I just made that up. There was only *one* man, wearing a stocking over his face."

"Well, it wasn't *me!*" Kahn shouted.

"Then who was it?" Brown shouted back. "You just said you learned about Albert Weinberg on the night of his murder. How?"

"The morning after, I meant. The newspapers . . ."

"You said 'the *night* of his murder,' you said you didn't even know he existed until that night. How'd you find *out* about his existence, Mr. Kahn? From my open notebook by the telephone?"

"Just a second, just a second," Petitpas shouted.

"I didn't kill him!" Kahn shouted.

"What'd you do, go after him the minute you left me?"

"No!"

"Just a second!"

"Walk the three blocks to his room . . ."

"No!"

"You killed him, Kahn, admit it!"

"No!"

"You attacked me . . ."

"Yes, no, NO!"

"Yes or no?"

Kahn had half-risen from his chair, and now he collapsed back into it, and began sobbing.

"Yes or no, Mr. Kahn?" Carella asked gently.

"I didn't want to . . . to hit you, I deplore violence,"

Kahn said, sobbing, not looking up at Brown. "I intended
only to . . . to force you to give me the piece you had
. . . to . . . to threaten you with the gun. And then . . .
when you opened the door, I . . . you looked so *big* . . .
and . . . and in that split second, I . . . I decided to . . .
to strike out at you. I was very frightened, so frightened.
I . . . I was afraid you might hurt me."

"Book him," Brown said. "First Degree Assault."

"Just a second," Petitpas said.

"Book him," Brown said flatly.

11

IT WAS time to put on that old thinking cap.

It was time for a little plain and fancy deduction.

Nothing can confuse a person (cops included) more than a lot of names and a lot of pieces and a lot of corpses. Stop any decent law-abiding citizen on the street and ask him which he would prefer, a lot of names and pieces and corpses or a simple hatchet murder, and see what he says. Oh, you can safely bet six-to-five he'll take that hatchet in the head any day of the week, Thursday included, and Thursdays are no prizes, except when they fall on Thanksgiving.

Here's the way they saw it.

Fact: Renninger killed Ehrbach and Ehrbach killed Renninger—a simple uncomplicated mutual elimination, which was only fair.

Fact: Bramley Kahn kayoed Arthur Brown in one point four seconds of the first round, using the .32 Smith & Wesson Brown later found in the bottom drawer of Kahn's desk, and using as well his own feet—not for nothing was Kahn renowned as one of the fanciest dancers in gay bars all along The Quarter's glittering Kublenz Square.

Fact: Somebody killed Albert Weinberg.

NOT NECESSARILY SIGNIFICANT.

Fact: Somebody killed Geraldine Ferguson.

NOT NECESSARILY SIGNIFICANT.

(The "somebody," it was decided after intensive questioning was definitely *not* Bramley Kahn, who had gone directly home to the arms of a forty-four-year-old closet queen after battering Brown senseless.)

Fact(s): There were seven names on the list in Carmine Bonamico's handwriting. Carmine had skillfully dissected the list, giving one-half of it to his late wife,

126

Alice Bonamico, and the other half to his late mistress, Geraldine Ferguson. Thoughtful fellow he, sharing his bed, his board, and also his contemplated ill-gotten gains with the two fairest flowers in his life. More's the pity the two broads could not have put their heads and their halves together and thereafter reaped the rewards of Carmine's professional acumen. Crime does not pay if you're fooling around with another woman.

Fact(s): There were eight pieces to the picture that revealed the location of the N.S.L.A. loot. Carmine had given two pieces to each of his associates, and had presumably kept two pieces for himself, he being the founder and beloved leader of the doomed band of brigands.

Fact: Petey Ryan, a gun on the ill-fated caper, had given one of his pieces to Dorothea McNally, woman about town, and another to Robert Coombs, restaurateur extraordinaire.

Fact: Lou D'Amore, the second gun, had given one of his pieces to Geraldine Ferguson, art appreciator, and the other to Donald Renninger, ex-cellmate.

Fact: Carmine Bonamico, mastermind, had given one of his pieces to Alice, his aforementioned wife.

Theory: Was it possible that Jerry Stein, Jewish driver of the misbegotten getaway car, had given one of his pieces to Albert Weinberg, and another to Eugene Edward Ehrbach, both of them likewise Jewish, rather than handing them over, say, to some passing Arab? NOT NECESSARILY SIGNIFICANT.

Question: To whom had Carmine Bonamico given the eighth piece of the picture, the piece for which no name had been listed?

Or (to break things down into list form, which the police were very fond of doing):

PETE RYAN	-- DOROTHEA MCNALLY	(1)
	ROBERT COOMBS	(2)
LOU D'AMORE	-- GERALDINE FERGUSON	(3)
	DONALD RENNINGER	(4)
JERRY STEIN	-- ALBERT WEINBERG-?	(5)
	EUGENE E. EHRBACH-?	(6)
CARMINE BONAMICO	-- ALICE BONAMICO	(7)
	?????????????????	(8)

But there was more, oh there was yet more, a policeman's lot is not a happy one. For example, was it not Irving Krutch, the *provocateur*, who had told the police that Alice Bonamico's piece, together with a torn list of names, had been willed to her sister, Lucia Feroglio, from whose dainty Sicilian hands Krutch had acquired both items, having faithlessly promised that good lady a thousand dollars in return for them? And had he not also said that Lucia had told him the assembled photograph would reveal the location of "*il tesoro,*" and had not Lucia delicately denied ever having said this to him? Or, for that matter, ever having given him a list of names? Ah so. And if he had *not* received his information from Lucia, then from whom exactly had it come? The person in possession of the eighth piece? The person who had gone unlisted by Carmine Bonamico?

On the night of Weinberg's murder, Brown had talked to three people: his wife Caroline, whom he could safely discount as a suspect; Weinberg, himself, who had been speedily dispatched to that great big photo lab in the sky; and Irving Krutch, to whom he had reported having struck pay dirt with Weinberg.

It seemed about time to talk to Irving Krutch again. If Krutch was lying about having received the list of names from Lucia Feroglio, he could also be lying about having spent that night of the murder in his apartment with Suzanne Endicott. It was worth a try. When you're running out of suspects, it's even worth talking to the local Welsh terrier. Brown put on his sunglasses in preparation for the insurance investigator's dazzling smile.

Krutch was not smiling.

"The old bag's lying," he said. "It's as simple as that."

"Or maybe you are," Brown said.

"Why should I be? For Christ's sake, I'm the one who *came* to you with all this stuff. I'm as anxious to locate that money as you are. It's my *career* here that's at stake, don't you realize that?"

"Okay, I'll ask you again," Brown said patiently. "Why would a nice old deaf lady who hardly speaks English and who's incidentally waiting for you to fork over a thousand bucks . . ."

"I'll pay her, don't you worry. Krutch doesn't welsh."

"Why would this nice old lady deny having told you anything about a treasure? Or about having given you a list of names?"

"How do I know? Go ask *her*. I'm telling you she gave

me the list, a piece of the picture, and the information
that tied them together."

"She says she only gave you the picture."

"She's a liar. Sicilians are liars."

"Okay, Krutch," Brown said, and sighed. "One other
thing I'd like to know."

"What's that?"

"I want to know where you were on Monday night
when Geraldine Ferguson got killed."

"What? Why the hell do you want to know *that?*"

"Because we'd already told you we struck out on
Gerry's safe. And maybe you decided to have a look
around her apartment, the way you've had a look around
a few other apartments."

"No," Krutch said, and shook his head. "You've got
the wrong customer."

"Okay, so tell me where you were."

"I was in bed with Suzanne Endicott."

"You're *always* in bed with Suzanne Endicott, it seems."

"Wouldn't *you* be?" Krutch said, and flashed his brilliant grin.

"And, of course, she'll corroborate that."

"Go ask her. I've got nothing to hide," Krutch said.

"Thanks, partner," Brown said.

When he got back to the squadroom, Carella told him
that there had been a call from Bramley Kahn, who had
been arraigned, released on bail, and—while awaiting
trial—was back selling art at the same old stand. Brown
returned his call at once.

"I want to talk a deal," Kahn said.

"I'll be right over," Brown answered.

When he got to the gallery, Kahn was waiting in his
office, seated in the old-fashioned swivel chair behind his
desk, facing the painting of the nude on the wall opposite.
Brown took a seat in one of the leather-and-chrome
chairs. Kahn took a long time getting started. Brown
waited. At last, Kahn said, "Suppose . . ." and hesitated.

"Yes, suppose what?"

"Suppose I know where Gerry's piece of the picture
is?"

"Do you?"

"I'm saying suppose."

"Okay, suppose you do?"

"Suppose I didn't tell you everything I know about that
picture?"

"Okay, go ahead, we're still supposing."

"Well, what would it be worth to you?"

"I can't make any promises," Brown said.

"I understand that. But you *could* talk to the district attorney, couldn't you?"

"Oh, sure. He's a very nice fellow, the D.A., always eager for a little chat."

"I've heard that the D.A.'s office is the bargain basement of the law," Kahn said. "Well, I want a bargain."

"Your lawyer pleaded 'Not Guilty' to Assault One, didn't he?"

"That's right."

"Okay, let's suppose you're willing to co-operate, and let's suppose I can catch the D.A.'s ear, and let's suppose he allowed you to plead guilty to a lesser charge, how would that sound to you?'

"A lesser charge like what?"

"Like Assault Two."

"What's the penalty for that?"

"A maximum of five years in prison, or a thousand-dollar fine, or both."

"That's steep," Kahn said.

"The penalty for Assault One is even steeper."

"What is it?"

"A maximum of ten years."

"Yes, but Anatole feels I can win my case."

"Anatole's dreaming. You confessed to the crime in the presence of your own lawyer, four detectives, and a police stenographer. You haven't got a chance in hell of beating this rap, Kahn."

"Still, he feels we can do it."

"In which case, I would suggest that you change your lawyer."

"How about *Third* Degree Assault? Is there such a thing?"

"Yes, there is, but forget it. The D.A. wouldn't even listen to such a suggestion."

"Why not?"

"He's got a sure conviction here. He may not even want to reduce it to Second Degree. It all depends on how valuable your information is. And on whether or not he had a good breakfast on the morning I go to talk to him."

"I think my information is *very* valuable," Kahn said.

"Let me hear it, and I'll tell you how valuable it is."

"First, what's the deal?"

"I told you, I can't make any promises. If I think

your information is really worth something, I'll talk to the D.A. and see what he thinks. He may be willing to accept a plea of guilty to Assault Two."

"That sounds very nebulous."

"It's all I've got to sell," Brown said, and shrugged. "Yes or no?"

"Suppose I told you . . ." Kahn said, and hesitated.

"I'm listening."

"Let's start with the picture."

"Okay, let's start with the picture."

"There are eight pieces, right?"

"Right."

"But only seven names on the list."

"Right."

"Suppose I know where that eighth piece went?"

"Let's stop supposing," Brown said. *"Do* you know?"

"Yes."

"Okay, where'd it go? '

"To Alice Bonamico."

"We already know that, Kahn. Her husband gave her half of the list and one piece of the photograph. If that's all you're . . ."

"No, he gave her *two* pieces of the photograph."

"Two," Brown said.

"Two," Kahn repeated.

"How do you know?"

"Gerry tried to bargain with her, remember? But Alice was dealing from a position of strength. Her husband had given his *mistress* only half of the list. But to Alice, his *wife,* he had given the other half of the list plus two pieces of the photo. That can make a woman feel very important."

"Yes, that was very thoughtful of him," Brown said. He was remembering that Irving Krutch claimed to have received half of the list and only one piece of the picture from Lucia Feroglio. If Alice Bonamico had indeed possessed *two* pieces of the picture, why had she willed only *one* of those pieces to her sister? And where was the missing piece now, the eighth piece? He decided to ask Kahn.

"Where *is* that eighth piece now?" he asked.

"I don't know," Kahn said.

"Well, that's certainly very valuable information," Brown said. "When I talk to the D.A., he might even be willing to reduce the charge to Spitting On The Sidewalk, which is only a misdemeanor."

"But I *do* know where Gerry's piece is," Kahn said, unperturbed. "And believe me, it's a *key* piece. I don't think Bonamico realized how important a piece it was, or he wouldn't have entrusted it to a dumb gunsel like D'Amore."

"Okay," Brown said, "where *is* Gerry's piece?"

"Right behind you," Kahn said.

Brown turned and stared at the wall.

"We've already looked in the safe," he said.

"Not in the safe," Kahn said.

"Then where?"

"Give me a hand, will you?" Kahn said, and walked to the painting of the nude. Together, they lifted the painting from the wall, and placed it face-down on the rug. The canvas was backed with what appeared to be brown wrapping paper. Kahn lifted one corner of the backing and plucked a shining black-and-white scrap from where it was wedged between the frame and the canvas.

"Voilà," he said, and handed the scrap to Brown.

"Well," Kahn said, "what do you think now?"

"I think you're right," Brown answered. "It *is* a key piece."

It was a key piece because it gave perspective to the photograph. There was no sky, they now realized, because the picture had been taken from *above,* the photographer shooting *down* at what now revealed itself as a road running beside a footpath. The Donald Duck segment of the picture, now that the perspective was defined, showed three benches at the back of the fowl's head, a broken patch in the cement forming the bird's eye, a series of five fence posts running vertically past its bill. The bill jutted out into . . .

Not mud, not cement, not stucco, not fur, but *water.* Cool, clear water.

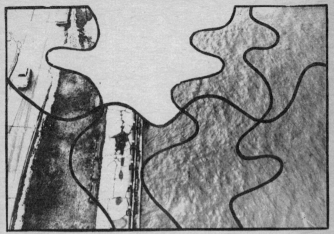

Or, considering the fact that Carmine Bonamico and his inept band had tried to make their escape along the River Road, perhaps water that was *not* quite so clear, perhaps water that was slightly polluted, but water nonetheless, the water of the River Dix that ran along the southern bank of Isola. Carella and Brown had a hurried conversation in the squadroom, and decided between them that Donald Duck should be easy to spot from the air.

He was not all that easy to spot.

They boarded a police helicopter at the heliport downtown and flew above the River Road for close to three hours, up and down its winding length, swooping low wherever a side street entered the road. The upper left-hand corner of the picture indicated just such a side street entering *somewhere*, and they hoped now to find the elusive duck with its telltale eye just below one of those entrances. The footpath with its benches and its guardrail ran the length of the river. There were thirty-four side streets entering the road, spaced at ten-block intervals. Their only hope of finding the *right* side street was to find the broken patch of cement.

But the robbery had taken place six years ago.

And whereas the city was sometimes a trifle slow in repairing broken sections of footpaths, they had done a damn good job on Donald Duck's eye.

Without the missing eighth piece, nobody knew where *nothing* was.

12

You CAN sometimes solve a mystery by the simple proc-
ess of elimination, which is admittedly undramatic, but
where does it say that a cop has to get hit on the head
every day of the week? Cops may be dumb, but not
that dumb. When everything has already narrowed itself
down into the skinny end of the funnel, when nearly
everybody's either dead or obviously innocent, then it
merely becomes a matter of trying to figure out who is
lying and why. There are lots of things cops don't understand, but lies they understand very well.

They don't understand, for example, why thieves will
spend so much time and energy devising and executing a
crime (with all its attendant risks) when that same
amount of time and energy devoted to a legal pursuit
would probably net much larger returns in the long run.
It was the belief of every detective on the 87th Squad
that the *real* motive behind half the crimes being committed in the city was *enjoyment,* plain and simple—the
fun of playing Cops and Robbers. Forget gain or profit
as motivation, forget passion, forget hostility or rebellion,
it all came down to Cops and Robbers.

What had Carmine Bonamico been doing, if not playing
Cops and Robbers? Took his little camera, dear boy,
and went out to photograph the River Road from an air-
plane or something, and then drew his squiggly little
lines across the print, and cut it apart, and handed out
pieces to his gang, all hush-hush, top-secret, tip-toey,
clever-crook stuff—Cops and Robbers. Why the hell

hadn't he just whispered the location to each of his hoods, and asked them to whisper it in turn to their friends and loved ones? Ah, but no. That would have taken from the crime one of its essential elements, known to gumshoes far and wide as The Game Aspect. Take the fun out of criminal activity, and all the prisons in the world would be empty. Who can figure crooks? Certainly not cops. They couldn't even figure why Irving Krutch had had the audacity to come to them for assistance in locating the loot, unless this too was tied in with The Game Aspect, the sheer enjoyment of playing Cops and Robbers.

They *did* figure, however, that Krutch was not telling them the truth about his whereabouts on the nights Albert Weinberg and Geraldine Ferguson were murdered; when a man's lying, it comes over like a supersonic missile streaking through the atmosphere, and you don't have to be working for NASA to spot it. Krutch's alibi, of course, was a broad he'd been laying since the year One, hardly the most reliable sort of witness to bring to your defense in a courtroom. But Suzanne Endicott's credibility as a witness was academic unless they could get Krutch *into* a courtroom. Logical deduction aside, the fact remained that he claimed to have been in bed with Suzie while both murders were being committed, and Suzie backed his story, and it is quite a trick to be out killing people while you are home in your apartment making love to a sweet li'l ol' Georgia peach. These days, it was getting more and more difficult to arrest a person even if you caught him with a hacksaw in his bloody hands, standing over a dissected corpse. How could you arrest a mustache-twirling villain who had an alibi as long as a peninsula?

How indeed?

It was Carella who first got the idea.

He discussed it with Hawes, and Hawes thought it was too risky. Carella insisted that it was a good idea, considering the fact that Suzie Endicott was from Georgia. Hawes said he thought Brown might take offense if they even *suggested* the idea to him, and Carella said he thought Brown would go along with the idea wholeheartedly. Hawes protested that the notion was pretty far-out to begin with: Suzie had been living in the north for at least four years now, spending half that time in bed with Krutch (to hear her tell it), and had probably been pretty well assimilated into the culture; it was a bad idea. Carella informed Hawes that certain prejudices and stereotypes died very hard deaths, as witness Hawes' own reluctance to even *broach* the idea to Brown. Hawes took offense at that, saying he was as tolerant a man as ever lived, in fact it was his very tolerance that *caused* his reluctance, he simply didn't want to offend Brown by suggesting an idea that probably wouldn't work anyway. Carella raised his voice and demanded to know how they could possibly crack Suzie's story; *he* had tried to crack it, *Hawes* had tried to crack it, the only way they could get to her was to scare hell out of her. Hawes shouted that Brown's feelings were more important to him and to the well-being of the squad than solving any goddamn murder case, and Carella shouted back that prejudice was certainly a marvelous thing when a white man couldn't even explore an excellent idea with a Negro for fear of hurting his feelings.

"Okay, *you* ask him," Hawes said.

"I will," Carella answered.

They came out of the Interrogation Room together and walked to where Brown was sitting at his desk, studying the photograph for the seven-hundreth time.

"We've got an idea, Artie," Carella said.

"He's got an idea," Hawes said. "It's *his* idea, Artie."

"What's the idea?" Brown said.

"Well, you know," Carella said, "we're all pretty much agreed on this Krutch character, right?"

"Right."

"I mean, he wants that seven hundred and fifty G's so bad, his hands are turning green. And you can't tell me his *career* has anything to do with it."

"Me neither," Brown said.

"He wants that *money,* period. The minute he gets it, he'll probably take Suzie and head straight for Brazil."

"Okay, how do we get to him?" Brown asked.

"We go to Suzie."

"We've *been* to Suzie," Brown said. *"You* talked to her, *Meyer* talked to her, *Cotton* talked to her. She alibis Krutch right down the line."

"Sure, but she's been sleeping with the guy for four years," Hawes said, still annoyed by the thought.

"Another three years, and they're man and wife in the eyes of the law," Carella said. "You expect her *not* to back his alibis?"

"Okay, let's say she's lying," Brown said.

"Let's say she's lying. Let's say Krutch *did* leave that

apartment, once to kill Weinberg, and again to kill Gerry Ferguson."

"Okay, let's say it. How we going to prove it?"

"Well, let's say that we drop in on Krutch sometime tonight and ask him a few more questions. Just to keep him busy, you understand? Just to make sure he doesn't climb into the sack with li'l Suzie again."

"Yeah?"

"Yeah, and let's say about two o'clock in the morning, somebody knocks on li'l Suzie's door and starts getting rough with her."

"Come on, Steve, we can't do that," Brown said.

"I don't mean we actually push her around," Carella said.

"I told you he wouldn't buy it," Hawes said.

"I mean we just let her *think* we're getting rough."

"Well, why would she think that?" Brown asked. "If we're *not* going to push her around . . ."

"She's from Georgia," Carella said.

The squadroom went silent. Hawes looked at his shoes.

"Who's going to hit Krutch?" Brown asked.

"I thought Cotton and I might do that."

"And who'll go scare Suzie?"

The squadroom went silent again. The clock on the wall was ticking too loudly.

"Don't tell me," Brown said, and broke into a wide grin. "Man, I love it."

Hawes glanced at Carella uncertainly.

"You'll do it?" Carella said.

"Oh, man, I *love* it," Brown said, and fell into a deliberately broad dialect. "We goan send a big black nigger man to scare our Georgia peach out'n her skin! Oh, man it's delicious!"

Prejudice is a wonderful thing.

Stereotypes are marvelous.

At two o'clock in the morning, Suzie Endicott opened her door to find that the most terrifying of her Southern fantasies had materialized in the gloom, a Nigra come to rape her in the night, just as her mother had warned her time and again. She started to close the door, but her rapist suddenly shouted, "You jes' hole it right there, Missy. This here's the law! Detective Arthur Brown of d'87th Squad. I got some questions to ast you."

"Wh . . . wh . . . it's . . . the middle of the night," Suzie said.

Brown flashed his shield. "This hunk o' tin here doan

respec' no time o' day nor night," he said, and grinned.
"You goan let me in, Missy, or does I start causin' a
ruckus here?" Suzie hesitated. Brown suddenly wondered
if he were playing it too broadly, and then decided he
was doing just fine. Without waiting for an answer, he
shoved past her into the apartment, threw his fedora
onto the hall table, looked around appreciatively, whistled,
and said, "Man, this's *some* nice place you got here.
Ain't never *been* inside no fancy place like this one."

"Wh . . .wh . . . what did you want to ask me?" Suzie
said. She was wearing a robe over her nightgown, and
her right hand was clutched tightly into the collar of the
robe.

"Well now, ain' no hurry, is there?" Brown asked.

"I . . . I have to go to work in the mor . . . morning,"
Suzie said. "I . . . I . . . I . . . have to get some sleep," she
said, and realized instantly she had made a mistake by
even mentioning anything even remotely suggesting bed.
"I mean . . ."

"Oh, I *knows* whut you mean," Brown said, and
grinned lewdly. "Sit down, Missy."

"Wh . . . what did you want to ask?"

"I *said* sit down! You jes' do whut I tells you to do,
okay, an' we goan get along fine. Otherwise . . ."

Suzie sat instantly, tucking the flaps of her robe
around her.

"Those're nice legs," Brown said. He narrowed his
eyes. "Mighty fine white legs, I can tell you that, honey."

Suzie wet her lips and then swallowed. Brown was
suddenly afraid she might pass out cold before he got
to the finale of his act. He decided to push on regardless.

"We busted yo' li'l playmate half an hour ago," he
said. "So if you're thinkin *he* goan help you, you can
jes' f'get it."

"Who? What? What did you say?"

"Irving Krutch, yo' lover boy," Brown said. "You
shunt'a lied to us, Missy. That ain't goan sit too well
with the D.A."

"I didn't lie to . . . to . . . anybody," Suzie said.

"'Bout bein' in bed there all the time? 'Bout making
love there when two people was being murdered. Tsk,
tsk, Missy, them was outright lies. I'm really sprised
at you."

"We did, we were, we did do that, we . . ." Suzie
started, and realized they were talking about making

love, and suddenly looked into Brown's eyes, and saw the fixed, drooling stare of a sex-crazed maniac and wondered how she would ever get out of this alive. She should have listened to her mother who had warned her never to wear a tight skirt walking past any of these people because it was so easy to arouse animal lust in them.

"You in serious trouble," Brown said.

"I didn't . . ."

"Real serious trouble."

". . . lie to anybody, I swear."

"Only one way to get out of that trouble now," Brown said.

"But I didn't . . ."

"Only *one* way, Missy."

". . . really. I didn't lie, really. Really, officer," she heard herself saying to this black man, "officer, I really didn't, I swear. I don't know what Irving told you, but I honestly did not lie to anyone, if anyone was lying, it was him. I had no idea of anything, of it, of anything. I mean that, officer, you can check that out if you want to. I certainly wouldn't lie to the police, not to those nice policemen who . . ."

"Only *one* way to save yo' sweet ass now," Brown said, and saw her face go pale.

"Wh . . . what's that?" Suzie said. *"What* way? What?"

"You can tell d'troof," Brown said, and rose out of his chair to his full monstrous height, muscles bulging, eyes glaring, shoulders heaving, rose like a huge black gorilla, and hulked toward her with his arms dangling at his sides, hands curled like an ape's, towered over her where she sat small and white and trembling on the edge of her chair, and repeated in his most menacing nigger-in-the alley voice, "You can tell d'troof *now,* Missy, unless you cares to work it out some *other* way!"

"Oh my good Lord Jesus," Suzie shouted, "he left the apartment, he left both times, I don't know where he went, I don't know anything else, if he killed these people, I had nothing to do with it!"

"Thank you, Miss Endicott," Brown said. "Would you put on some clothes now, I'd like you to accompany me to the squadroom."

She stared at him in disbelief. Where had the rapist gone? Who was this polite nuclear physicist standing in his place? And then his charade dawned upon her, and her eyes narrowed, and her lips drew back over her teeth, and she said, "Boy, you say *please* when you ask *me* to go any place."

"Go to *hell*," Brown said. "Please."

"The rotten bitch," Krutch said.

He could have been talking about Suzie Endicott, but he wasn't. He was railing, instead, against the late Alice Bonamico. The departed gang leader's departed wife, it seemed, had cheated Krutch. In his investigation of the robbery, he had learned from Carmine's widow that she was in possession of "certain documents and photographic segments" purporting to show the hiding place of the N.S.L.A. loot. He had bargained with her for months, and they had finally agreed on a purchase price. She had turned over to him the half of the list in her possession as well as the piece of the photo he had originally shown the police.

"But I didn't know she had yet *another* piece," Krutch said. "I didn't learn that until I read about her will, and contacted her sister. That's when I got *this* piece. The eighth piece of the puzzle. The *important* one. The one that bitch held out on me."

"Which, naturally, you didn't give to us," Brown said.

"Naturally. It shows the exact location of the loot. Do you think I'm an idiot?"

"Why'd you come to us in the first place?"

"I *told* you why. Krutch needed help. Krutch couldn't handle it alone any more. Krutch figured what better way to get help on an investigation than by calling in experts?"

"You got more than you bargained for," Brown said.

"Except from Alice Bonamico, that bitch. I paid her ten thousand dollars for half of the list and a meaningless piece of the picture. Ten thousand bucks! It was every penny I had."

"But, of course, you were going for very big money."

"It was an investment," Krutch said. "Krutch looked upon it as an investment."

"Well," Brown said, "now Krutch can look upon it as a capital loss. Why'd you kill Weinberg?"

"Because you told me he had another piece, and I wanted it. Look, I was running a race with you guys. I knew I was ahead of you because *I* had the piece with the X on it, but suppose you got cute somewhere along the line and refused to show me anything else? I'm in the insurance business, you know. Getting Weinberg's piece was insurance, plain and simple."

"And Gerry Ferguson's?"

"Same thing. Insurance. I went in there looking for it because you'd already told me it wasn't in the safe. So where *else* could it be? Had to be in her apartment, right? I wasn't going to kill her, but she started screaming the minute I came in. I was too close then to let anybody stop me. You don't *know* how close I came to putting this whole thing together. You guys were helping me more than you realized. I almost had it made."

"You've got balls, all right," Brown said, shaking his head. "You come to the police for help in locating the proceeds from a bank robbery. That takes real balls."

"Real *brains*," Krutch corrected.

"Oh, yes," Brown said.

"It wasn't easy to think this up."

"You'll have plenty of time to do a lot more thinking," Brown said.

"What do you mean?"

"You figure it out."

"In prison, do you mean?" Krutch asked.

"Now you've got the picture," Brown said.

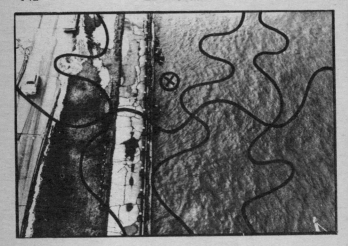

This time, the helicopter ride was a joyous one. For whereas there were thirty-four side streets entering the River Road, only one of those side streets was opposite a twin cluster of offshore rocks. Coincidentally, the rocks were just west of the Calm's Point Bridge, from which vantage point Bonamico must have snapped the picture, standing on the bridge's walkway some fifty feet above the surface of the water. They landed the chopper close to where Donald Duck's eye must have been before the city's Highway Maintenance Department had repaired it, and then they walked toward the rocks and looked down into the filthy waters of the River Dix and saw nothing. Carmine Bonamico's "X" undoubtedly marked the spot, but water pollution triumphed over the naked eye, and there was nary a treasure to be seen. They did not uncover the loot until they dredged the river close to the bank, and found an old leather suitcase, green with slime, water-logged, badly deteriorated. Seven hundred and fifty thousand dollars in good American currency was ensconced in that bag, slightly damp to be sure, but nonetheless negotiable.

It was a good day's pay.

Arthur Brown got home in time for dinner.

His wife met him at the door and said, "Connie's got a fever. I had the doctor here a half-hour ago."

"What'd he say?"

"He thinks it's just the flu. But she's *so* uncomfortable, Artie."

"Did he give her anything?"

"I'm waiting for it now. The drug store said they'd deliver."

"She awake?"

"Yes."

"I'll go talk to her. How're *you?*" he said, and kissed her.

"Forgot what you looked like," Caroline answered.

"Well, here's what I look like," he said and smiled.

"Same old handsome devil," Caroline said.

"That's me," he said, and went into the bedroom.

Connie was propped against the pillows, her eyes wet, her nose running. "Hello, Daddy." she said in her most miserable-sounding voice.

"I thought you were sick," he said.

"I *am*," she answered.

"You can't be sick," he said, "you look too beautiful." He went to the bed and kissed her on the forehead.

"Oh, Daddy, please be careful," Caroline said, "you'll catch the bug."

"I'll catch him and stomp him right under my foot," Brown said, and grinned.

Connie giggled.

"How would you like me to read you a story?" he asked.

"Yes," she said. "Please."

"What would you like to hear?"

"A good mystery," Connie said. "One of the Nancy Drews."

"One of the Nancy Drews it is," Brown said, and went to the bookcase. He was crouched over, searching the shelves for Connie's favorite, when he heard the urgent shriek of a police siren on the street outside.

"Do you like mysteries, Daddy?" Connie asked.

Brown hesitated a moment before answering. The siren faded into the distant city. He went back to the bed and gently touched his daughter's hair, and wondered again, oddly, if Geraldine Ferguson had ever roller-skated on a city sidewalk. Then he said, "No, honey, I don't care for mysteries too much," and sat on the edge of the bed, and opened the book, and began reading aloud.

THINNING THE TURKEY HERD

A Jimmy Flannery Mystery
by Robert Campbell
Author of the Edgar Award-Winning *The Junkyard Dog*

Tough Chicago Irishman Jimmy Flannery has a nose for mayhem. As city sewer-inspector, he has to. So when a killer sets out to prune the year's crop of top models, Flannery is there to track the scent. But before he's through, gorgeous Joyce Lombardi disappears, an innocent man is lined up to take the fall for a powerful political bigwig, and Flannery begins to wonder if he has the stomach for it all . . .
